HOT DREAMS
(Book 1)

RACHELLE
CHASE

ISBN-10: 0-9864-2424-2
ISBN-13: 978-0-9864242-4-3

ACKNOWLEDGMENTS

This book truly could not have been written without the help of Leigh Michaels and Calista Fox. Not only is Leigh Michaels my friend and mentor, she made time to read and re-read, critique and critique again, all my chapters until I got them right. For years, Calista Fox repeatedly told me to finish this book. And when I picked it up again, Calista critiqued the early chapters, demanding more emotion until I gave it to her. If I've failed to deliver on their expert feedback, it is my fault, not theirs.

Special thanks to my niece for being the inspiration behind Brianna, Muhammad Wong for introducing me to *Cyrano de Bergerac*, Michael Lemberger for helping me decipher the pool terms (I take full responsibility for "bed of the table" and any and all errors), and to my readers who continue to read my books—especially those, like Julie Beagle, who prod me to write by asking, "When's your next book coming out?"

As usual, I give all my love and dedicate this book to my family for always believing in me.

1

Tina stared at his naked body, unable to look away. He stood bare-chested, his bronze skin seeming to glow against the dark green fir trees in the background and brighten the gray day. His legs were parted, the muscles tense, his bare toes digging into the grass, as his fingers dug into the denim-covered ass of the woman whose legs were wrapped around his waist. Her head was thrown back, strands of long blonde hair nearly brushing his fingers as her breasts strained against her tight pink t-shirt, the hard nipples seeming to seek his mouth, inches away.

Tina set the plastic watering can on the glass-top credenza and held the photo in both hands. She ran her fingertip over the image of the man's chest, tracing the muscle, wondering if he was cold, wearing nothing but a skimpy thong under the gloomy sky.

Liar.

Okay. So that wasn't even close to what she was thinking.

Instead, she wanted to know if his chest felt like

satin-covered steel and what it would be like to be gripped by his large hands. To *be* the woman in the photo, to be held by that mouth-wateringly gorgeous man, to be pressed against his hips, the feel of him searing her skin through the denim, making her wet.

Not that the woman in the photo was wet. For her, it was probably no big deal to be in the arms of yet another hunky man. With the smooth, tight skin surrounding her emerald eyes and her flawless complexion, she could probably have any man she wanted.

Tina raised a hand to her own face, running her fingers along her jaw line and up over her cheek, then around her eye, rubbing skin that felt as flawless as the blonde's looked. And without a mirror, Tina could pretend that it was.

She dropped her hand and forced her gaze from the photograph she was holding. She stared at the other photos decorating the credenza. In each one, the man appeared with a woman of a different race— white, black, East Indian, Asian, Latina, and several she couldn't identify. Sometimes, the woman stood with one leg thrown across his torso, with his strong fingers gripping her thigh. Other times, she straddled him upright like the blonde in the first photo.

In every image, the man's smile was the same— masculine, confident, as if he was used to women wanting him, as if he was used to fulfilling their sinful desires.

But his smile didn't say what *he* wanted. Nor did his eyes. While enthusiasm and attraction shone from the women's, his toffee-colored irises remained impersonal.

Sexy, but shuttered. Distant.

Did real enthusiasm and attraction ever shine there?

Maybe that was the appeal he held for Tina, why she stood staring at his pictures, aroused by his raw masculinity—the bunch of his muscles as he gripped a waist or an ass or a thigh, the self-confidence he oozed for the camera—while drawn to the . . . *nothingness* . . . that seemed to lurk behind the sexy smile. No glimmer of heat. No flicker of passion. No hint of emotion.

Maybe, like her, he felt those things but had to hide them.

He hid them because he had to remain professional. She hid them because it was best not to show desire for things she would never have, never experience.

Maybe, in that way, they were kindred spirits.

Yeah, right.

She frowned. "Maybe you should just stick to things you know. Like plants."

Exactly. What was wrong with her tonight? Rarely did she take interest in the offices she entered. All she'd ever cared about before were the plants—removing a dead leaf here, wiping away dust there, speaking to them softly to spur good health, while supplying the water and food necessary for a prolonged life. Plants responded to her touch and flourished under her care, totally accepting, never judging. She loved them, and this love, along with her ability to nurture, were traits that ensured her business, Plants Alive, thrived and continued to keep and attract new clients.

New clients like this one, Hot Dreams.

An appropriate name for a male entertainment

company, for she had been dreaming and she did, indeed, feel hot.

Tina set the photo aside and reached for the Pothos plant in the matte gray pot. But, as she tilted the watering can toward its dry soil, she couldn't stop wondering what the sexy man in the photo felt.

~~~~

Johnny Guerra stared at Club Boudoir's stage, which was currently being used as a dance floor. Lights flashed, in sync with the pounding bass in the music and the squeaking bedsprings sound effects, while Wale, Rihanna and Ludacris sang the virtues of bad girls. The lights brought the dancers into sharp relief, then cast them in shadows, making their movements look more frenzied than they actually were.

But Johnny's gaze barely registered the dancers on stage, just as he barely noticed the dancers around him, occasionally jostling, sometimes shouting their agreement with the lyrics that bad girls had all the fun.

Instead, he took in the spotlights overhead, imagining his guys on the stage against a Caribbean backdrop, with beams of white light trained on them. Palm trees would line the sides and hidden fans would rustle the fronds of the trees and the men's hair, along with their tropical shirts and white shorts. When they were wearing them, anyway.

Yeah, they could do the Caribbean Nights routine at Club Boudoir.

He turned and looked at the crowd—actually, *through* the crowd—picturing them replaced by chairs. No, not chairs. Theatre-type, tiered seating that could be rolled in and out of place quickly, seating several hundred. The club was smaller than he liked, but Hot

Dreams' take of the door cover, in addition to their performance fee, would make up for it.

His gaze circled the crowd, this time looking *at* them. Or more specifically, at the women. Because they were his target market.

Twenty- to early thirty-somethings. Sexy smiles. Excessive hair tossing and twirling. Mounds of cleavage. Micro-minis. All melting into a sea of bare skin and gyrating hips, oftentimes within inches from their male partners'. Or clusters of women dancing together, hip-to-hip, tits-to-tits, stoking the woman-on-woman or me-and-two-babes sex fantasies of the clumps of guys watching.

Yeah, definitely a Hot Dreams, girls-just-want-to-have-fun crowd.

Brandon Evans had done good, pitching the idea for an opening show there, a prime-the-pump kind of thing, where they drew the women in and got them all riled up, which then brought in the men. Not a new idea, but new to Hot Dreams since Johnny had been too busy to pursue it. Brandon had management potential, if he could get his marriage under control and focus on work.

Having seen all he needed to, Johnny threaded his way across the floor, moving through the dancers and headed toward the exit. Halfway there, two women blocked his path. A busty one with straight brown hair wore what looked like a silky shorts lingerie set, while the curvy redhead wore a skintight blue dress that barely reached her thighs. Both smiled and circled him, tossing their long hair, waving their slender arms in the air, and gyrating their hips to 50 Cent's *In Da Club*.

They sandwiched him. One ass brushed his. The

other brushed against his cock.

At one time, Johnny would have gone into Hot Dreams mode—his term for when, if he was interested, he became the flatterer, the seducer, the aggressor, or whatever the woman expected him to be, as long as they shared the same goal: Sex. And only sex.

The brunette looped her hands around his neck, drawing his attention to her. He gazed into her brown eyes, framed by long mascara-coated lashes and dark eye shadow. They were half-closed, gazing up at him with a smoky bedroom look. The tip of her tongue slowly circled her glossy lips, as if she was acting along as 50 Cent began rapping about licking lollipops that had nothing to do with candy. Overall, her looks were average, though her use of makeup accented her strengths—the roundness of her eyes, the cinnamon brown color of her skin.

Johnny's gaze drifted lower. Her tits were smaller than he liked, but they bounced freely under the silky top and their movement beneath the silk enticed more than a clingy t-shirt with a plunging v-neck would have. Her hips were slimmer than he preferred, but the silky material draped, rather than hugged, and she knew how to use them, swiveling and swirling them fluidly, as she kept time to the Middle Eastern notes undulating through the lyrics.

Taken as a package, there was nothing physically remarkable about her. But what made her hot was her attitude, her confidence. And the way she kept inching her body closer, centimeters away from grinding against him, he'd bet she was game for more than a dance.

Yeah, at one time, he would have gone into

Dreams mode. But not tonight. In fact, Johnny couldn't remember the last time he'd felt the urge to. Nowadays, he put those skills to use at Hot Dreams, which after thirteen years of hard work, was getting noticed nationwide for his efforts, for being different. Unlike other male dance companies, his guys didn't just come onto the stage, strip off their clothes and lead some giggling or squealing woman onto the stage for an air fuck. They seduced. They teased. They gave visual foreplay. They created a fantasy in which the women watching believed they were the star. And Johnny was proud of that.

He reached into his inside jacket pocket and removed a card. Unlacing her hands from around his neck, he placed the card for their upcoming show in her palm and flashed her a grin and a wink.

His smile immediately disappeared as he moved away and continued toward the exit.

"Hey, Johnny."

He turned in the direction of the familiar voice, his gaze connecting with the woman seated at the bar. Her blonde hair was artfully highlighted, as if acquired from the sun instead of an overpriced salon. Her skin was porcelain smooth and blemish-free, compliments of a leading dermatologist. Dark eyeliner accentuated her eyes, giving their slightly almond shape an even sexier lilt. Her perfectly-shaped lips, the top slightly plumper than the bottom, were painted a rose color that glistened under the soft overhead light.

No need for *her* to run her tongue around her lips to 50 Cent's lyrics of lollipops and magic sticks. Johnny knew firsthand what she could do with her mouth.

His cock twitched at the memory.

He walked to the bar. "Hi, Catherine." He bent down to kiss her cheek, catching the tangy floral scent of her perfume.

"Thought you didn't do clubs. What brings you here?"

"Business."

"Ahh, but of course. All done?"

"Yeah."

She raised her martini glass to her lips and took a sip. "Then let me buy you a drink."

"Thanks. But not tonight."

"Well then." Her voice dropped to a husky purr. A red-tipped finger lightly circled the rim of her glass, reminding him that she'd been good with her hands, too. "Let's skip the drinks."

Like the woman on the dance floor, Catherine was confident. But in a classier, more seductive way, which sexually stimulated the brain as well as the body. And unlike the woman on the dance floor, he wouldn't have to seduce, flirt, or flatter Catherine. Nor guess what she wanted. He already knew.

She was sexy, hot, and insatiable. They'd fucked against the wall, on the floor and on the table, before finally making their way to her bed, where they'd fucked again. There'd been no pillow talk or any talk, other than what mattered. Like "Fuck me harder" or "Faster" or "Don't stop." There'd been no thinking about anything, other than how to satisfy and be satisfied. There'd been no feeling, other than the satiny feel of her skin or the way her pussy clenched his cock. And when they were done, there was no spooning off to sleep. Instead, she'd said goodbye with a kiss and a smile and a "Let's do it again sometime."

And they had. Several mind-blowing sometimes.

She was one of the—if not THE—best fucks of his life. She kept him so busy fucking, there was no room for thoughts or feelings of what he'd give anything—and give up everything—to undo.

He stared into her eyes, eyes that had already gone dark and sultry as if she, too, was remembering their last time.

She was ready.

His cock was ready.

But he wasn't in the mood. Hadn't been in the mood for awhile. Not even for the moment of escape it would provide.

"Not tonight. Gotta work."

She tsked. "A pity."

His cock agreed.

You don't have *to work. What the hell is wrong with you?*

If only he knew.

~~~~

On her way out, Tina took a final look at the plants. The areca palm trees outside the conference room and the weeping fig near the reception desk glistened. Not a brown leaf was in sight on the delicate Boston ferns along the wall. As she passed the hunk's office, she cast a loving glance at the Pothos, pleased at the way its healthy leaves shone in the fluorescent light. Her gaze dropped to the credenza and she gasped in dismay. There sat the photo she'd been ogling, two feet away from the others.

What if she'd left without noticing? How would she have explained it? For, given the lack of clutter in his office, the not-a-paper-in-sight desk, she was sure he'd notice. And who, besides the cleaning people, would be pegged for having done it?

Entering the room, she picked up the photo, removed her dust rag and traced the smudges made with her finger, clearing them with the rag. With the realization that the smudges were gone and she was still fondling his image, Tina shook her head in disgust and bent to return the photo to its place on the credenza.

Lesson learned. She was not going to touch a single photo the next time she was in.

"What the hell are you doing?" demanded a deep voice from behind her.

She jumped as a sharp cry burst from her lips. As she pivoted toward his voice, the frame flew out of her hand, crashed onto the desk, and splintered.

Her scream ended on a strangled note as she stared into the golden brown eyes of the man whose image she'd just been lusting after—whose arms she'd been imagining wrapped around her, whose muscles she'd fantasized about feeling, heating her through her jeans.

She felt the blood rush to her face as the palm of one hand instinctively flattened over her heart, which beat wildly. Catching her breath, she said, "You scared the hell out of me!"

Unlike the smiling cockiness reflected in the eyes of the photographed man, the real-life man stared back at her, his expression unreadable.

His gaze immediately snapped to her face.

Tina resisted the urge to cover herself as she imagined what he saw: Her hair pulled back from her face, drawing even more attention to the pink port-wine stain, even more livid with the blood flooding her face, that traced the left side from jaw to ear, then wound inward to touch the edge of her cheek before curving upwards to circle her eye.

She stiffened, waiting for the flash of surprise, the hint of revulsion, the flicker of pity, followed by avoidance, that nearly everyone seemed to show when they looked at her for the first time.

His gaze remained expressionless as it returned to her eyes.

Both eyes.

"Most people scare when they're guilty." Even sarcastic, his voice was the audio equivalent of standing under a chocolate fountain as the thick, warm liquid coated her body.

Though guilt seized her insides as she slid a glance at the shattered picture frame, she refused to let him intimidate her. Too much . . . "No, most people scare when someone sneaks up behind them."

He crossed his arms and leaned against the doorjamb, as if he had all night to wait for her answer.

His stare stunned her. Because he looked at her as if she were . . . normal. While her few close friends, her family, and of course her daughter, Brianna, looked at her like that, it was a new experience coming from a stranger. She'd always wished for it, but now that she'd gotten it, she wished that, like the others, he'd become uncomfortable and look away. Then she could be angered by the rejection.

But he didn't look discomfited. And she couldn't hide behind anger. Instead, she felt naked, vulnerable.

For the first time, *she* looked away.

Her gaze took in his loosened tie and royal blue shirt. Even to her untrained eye, the shirt appeared to be custom made: It fit the wide expanse of his chest without an unnecessary wrinkle and narrowed to follow his sides, before dipping into black slacks that draped his hips perfectly, revealing just the right hint of muscular thighs—

That was not helping.

She sucked in a sharp breath, attempting to curb her runaway thoughts.

Focus on business. That's what she needed to do. She'd just been caught red-handed by someone who employed her—and she'd broken one of his possessions! It was hard to think of a situation that could be worse for business.

Tina jerked around and scooped her watering can from the glass top, then turned back to him to explain what had really happened, lest he think she was some sort of stalker. Which he was probably used to, given his occupation and his sinfully gorgeous body. Still . . .

"I'm actually finished in here and was simply looking at your photos before leaving. I'm sorry for breaking that one. If you send Plants Alive the bill for the frame, I'll be more than happy to pay for it."

There. That sounded professional. So much so, that it might be enough to keep his business. Maybe. If she was lucky.

She took a step toward the door, intending to leave.

But how could she escape without making an even bigger fool of herself? While he wasn't totally blocking the exit, she'd have to turn sideways to get past him. Which would put her close enough to smell him, to inhale the unique scent of his skin. Her body would brush against his. Her breasts would probably rub up against his arm, making her nipples harden.

Tina stopped, not trusting herself to go forward. She wet her lips with her tongue. "If you'll excuse me, I'll let you get to work."

He pushed himself away from the doorway and stepped forward, stopping a mere foot or two in front of her. Close enough that the heat from his body caressed hers, just as she'd feared. His brown eyes snared her gaze, causing her breathing to become shallow as her lungs desperately tried to fan the heat beginning to burn through her body.

She forced herself to remain where she was standing, to ignore the pull toward him.

"You weren't 'simply looking' at my photos."

Tina's breaths turned jerky.

"You were touching them. Stroking them." His tone was neutral as he turned to his desk, removed the photo from beneath the broken glass, and swiveled back to her. He stared at the picture, running his finger along the chest that Tina had traced.

Oh God. He'd been standing there, watching her the whole time! Another rush of heat spread over her face.

"Why?" he asked in a low tone.

Face burning, blood raging, Tina gazed into his eyes. He wore the same shuttered expression she'd seen in the photos. The same look that had made her wonder if he ever felt anything, if he ever got any emotional enjoyment out of his interactions with those women.

The voice in her head urged her to smile and give him some flip answer to his question.

But his lack of revulsion and her need for an answer gave her the courage to tell the truth.

Pulling in a deep breath, Tina admitted, "I was

wondering what it would feel like to experience what none of those women had."

His lips twisted. "And what is that?"

"You," she said, her gaze unwavering. "The *real* you."

2

Johnny stared down at the woman in front of him, barely catching his mouth before it dropped open. For once, he wasn't feigning emotions he didn't feel for the benefit of a client. No, his surprise was genuine.

He hadn't expected her to say that. The way she'd run her fingers over his image, as if she'd been feeling his skin instead of mere glass, and the way she'd stood motionless as her fingers had stroked, her eyes riveted on the photo, had made him think that she'd wanted to fuck him. Maybe try some new position she'd read about in *Cosmo*. Or that she wanted to act out some fantasy that her boyfriend, girlfriend, husband, whoever, wouldn't engage in. Because that's what ninety-nine point nine percent of the women who had hired him to strip at birthday parties, bachelorette parties, going away parties, or no-reason parties wanted—despite the fact that he had made it crystal clear that he was a dancer, not a manwhore.

It had been his job to make women believe an

illusion—that they were the center of his universe. That every time his hands slid down his chest and over his abs, he was imagining *her* hands. And every gyration of his hips was in anticipation of thrusting between *her* thighs. He watched the women, analyzing their reaction to his moves and then adjusting his routine to include more of those that got them all worked up.

It was *never* personal. But he was good at making women believe that it was.

Or rather, he had been good, for he no longer danced. Instead, he left that to the men on staff and focused on creating and booking dance shows featuring his top guys. In the thirteen years that it had taken him to build the million-dollar male entertainment business, he thought he'd heard everything.

At thirty-one, he'd thought there was nothing left for a woman to ask for that would surprise him.

Until now.

I was wondering what it would feel like to experience what none of those women had—you. The real *you.*

Who the hell was she to even ask?

First, she was in *his* office, fingering *his* photos, and now, she spouted armchair psychology bullshit. He didn't have time for this. There was payroll to review, bills to reconcile, new dancers to hire.

And yet, bullshit or not, he had to know . . .

"And just how do you know that's not the real me?"

"Because your smile never reaches your eyes."

Her soft voice brought his attention back to her mouth. Her full, sensual lips curled into a self-conscious smile, causing dimples to appear in her cheeks made rosy by what he assumed was embarrassment.

The rosiness emphasized the healthy glow of the naturally smooth, flawless skin on one side, while darkening the other, turning the pink splotches a pale red.

The birthmark had been a surprise, second only to catching her in his office. But she'd been at an angle, her marked profile facing him, so he'd been able to study her, to notice that it covered part of her face from jaw to a bit of her cheek to some of her eye. The color wasn't solid, instead a Playboy-bunny-ears pink in some areas, a light mauve in others, interspersed with her natural skin color. The pattern was similar to a spirited Appaloosa horse he'd seen on a field trip to an Indian Reservation when he'd lived in the Arapahoe Group Home for Boys in Arizona.

So he'd been prepared when she'd faced him.

Fortunately.

Because when she'd turned toward him, after she'd gotten over *her* shock of seeing him and saw him looking at her, she'd jerked her head slightly to the left, straightened her shoulders, and lifted her chin. Her gaze had gone blank.

But not before he'd seen a flash of raw emotion that looked like a plea.

A plea for what?

He wasn't sure but given her defiant stance and the probably-unconscious jerking of her head, as if turning hid her, he guessed she was pleading for no reaction to her face, no *negative* reaction. Or maybe he was just projecting the feelings of Dwayne, his best friend at the Home, whose cleft lip and cleft palate had caused him to be equally defiant.

Returning his thoughts to her question, he said, "My eyes are hardly enough evidence to support your conclusion."

She took a deep breath, once again drawing his gaze to her chest. The clingy t-shirt traced and cupped her breasts, outlining her nipples, visible through the bra. But more importantly, the teardrop roundness of her breasts gave them a soft, natural look that Johnny never saw in those that had been surgically enhanced.

His balls tightened, surprising him. Yeah, sure, he had a thing for real breasts. But he'd seen a lot of them in his business and he was long past the age where a great pair, covered no less, gave him an instant hard-on.

And yet, he felt the beginnings of a hard-on.

"For me, they are. I can tell a lot from a person's eyes." She did that shoulder-straightening, chin-lifting thing again. "For example . . ." She turned back to his photos. While she reached forward, her hand hovering over one photograph before moving to the next, Johnny let his gaze drift over her. Her small waist gave way to rounded hips encased in tight pocketless jeans, her lush ass providing all the decoration they needed.

His cock thickened, making him uncomfortable.

Maybe I should've had that fuck-a-thon with Catherine, after all.

She pivoted around.

Johnny slowly returned his gaze to her face.

Though her cheeks reddened, the left turning even pinker, she made no comment. Instead, she turned the photo in her hands face out. In it, a Latina woman whose name he no longer remembered was propped against his hip, her arms looped around his neck, her thighs wrapped around his waist.

"She's hanging onto you, but you have only one hand resting lightly on her back, while the other hangs loosely at your side. You pose for the camera, making sure not to touch more than is necessary to hold the pose."

"It's business." Irritation at having to state the obvious wrapped itself around the words. "I leave clients with a memento of the performance, not an invitation to a sexual harassment lawsuit."

"Exactly. And all I'm saying is that it shows—in your eyes and in your body language—that you're physically and emotionally detached. In this photo." Her hand gestured behind her to the others on the credenza. "And all of those." She paused and nibbled her lip, distracting him. "That's what made me wonder if you were physically and emotionally detached in real life. And, if not, what it would be like to experience the real you and . . ."

The flare of interest Johnny had felt instantly faded. He could finish the sentence for her: . . . and therefore be *the* one and only woman to experience the 'real' him. Which meant that she, like the others, wanted a trophy for her mantel.

He felt an irrational flicker of disappointment. And after it came the shocking realization of why she'd piqued his curiosity in the first place. Because she'd had the audacity, the confidence, to stand in his office and make assumptions about him, without backing down.

Her assumptions were wrong—he *was* emotionally detached, emotionally dead—but she'd made assumptions that made him seem . . . better than he really was.

He kinda liked that.

At that thought, irritation flashed through him.

What kind of sappy-shit thinking was that?

No, that was *not* the reason she'd caught his interest. He didn't want her—or any woman—thinking there was more of anything to him. He liked being viewed as an object. He *needed* to be viewed as an object. It kept business simple, his intimate 'relationships' superficial, and memories of another life at bay.

No, it was her boldness—the audacity of riffling through his stuff, then justifying it with curiosity—that intrigued him. He liked boldness in a woman, especially if it spilled over into bed.

She continued. "Your emotional detachment made me wonder what a woman would have to do to make your smile heartfelt. What would she have to be like to attract you?"

Okay, so he was wrong. Again. *That* was definitely different.

This woman was making his head spin, never saying what he expected. Just like Marta.

The familiar jolt of pain zapped his chest in the space that used to house his heart.

Jonathon, it was not your fault.

The familiar burst of anger at the therapist's words rushed through his mind.

Johnny took a deep breath, erasing the empty words that were meant to make him feel better.

Nothing made him feel better about the past. Except *not* feeling. Just filling his life with work, success, and the occasional round of mind-numbing sex.

He returned his attention to the woman in front of

him. To her green eyes staring back at him as if she was trying to see into his soul, as if he had one. Her eyes reminded him of that famous photo of the Afghan girl that had appeared on the cover of *National Geographic* magazine decades ago but still circled the Internet. Not so much the color, but rather the intensity. Just as the girl's golden skin tone and the earthy colors surrounding her eyes had made them even more stunning, the cotton candy pink stain that circled this woman's left eye, while leaving the right bare, emphasized the intensity shining in both.

The intensity of the Afghan girl's gaze had been beautiful yet painful, compelling yet discomfiting.

Just like hers.

He shifted his gaze to safer territory. To the kiss-me lips that seemed to be parted in expectation of an answer to the question that still hung in the air.

Well, she could wonder all she wanted. *He* didn't want a woman to make his smile heartfelt. *He* didn't want a woman to attract him, unless it was for sex.

Forcing the disturbing thoughts from his mind, Johnny slipped back into his *real* skin. Where he was viewed as an object—and he viewed women as objects.

This was the only 'him' there was now, the only 'him' any woman would ever see.

He let his gaze drift lower, over her slim hips and jean-clad thighs, to her white-tipped toenails. He took his time, imagining the soft skin hidden by the clothing—skin that he could caress until it quivered, muscles he could stroke until they clenched.

He pictured her naked thighs wound around his hips. On cue, his cock got hard. He smiled, forcing the lust and heat throbbing in his body to shine in his eyes.

"Does *this* smile reach my eyes?"

She gasped.

With her response, the last bit of discomfort faded away. He was firmly back on familiar ground.

He let seduction leak into his smile and took a step closer. One deep breath and his chest would touch hers. Her nipples would rake his skin, sending a blaze of heat through him despite the fabric. "Does it let you know that I'm attracted to you?"

The lust flashing in her irises faded.

Johnny wanted her lust back. He resisted the urge to trail his finger along the curve of her jaw before letting it slip to her neck, moving inward, feeling the jerky pulse he could see beating against his flesh. He sensed that any touch, the barest caress, would send her into fits of distrust, not arousal.

"I believe that you are . . ." She licked her lips, causing another jerk of his cock. "I believe you can turn your attraction on and off, summon thoughts at will that'll convey a certain look."

She was right. Hadn't he just proven that?

"That's what you do when you dance, isn't it? But is it really me? Are you really attracted to *me*?" Disdain oozed from her voice. "No."

"Yes," Johnny said. Though his voice was soft, pitched to soothe and seduce, his answer surprised him. Because it was true, despite the fact that she wasn't his type. And not because of the birthmark.

Sure, her blemish had been unexpected, especially contrasted to the wholesome prettiness of the other side of her face. But its imperfection, a profusion of color that wove along her skin, partially framing the curve of her sexy eyes, emphasized the perfection of the untouched skin, the beauty of her features. A sort of yin and yang that spilled over into her actions— guarded and open, defiant and unsure—creating a complexity and depth that didn't exist in the women he surrounded himself with. But when combined with her hot body, it intrigued and attracted him.

His attraction shocked him because he didn't do 'complex' and 'depth.' And even worse, the words he had used to describe her face—'wholesome' and 'untouched'—went beyond the physical, giving *her* an innocent vibe.

Innocence was not fuckable.

That was the reason she wasn't his type. Johnny avoided innocence and complexity like demons avoided holy water.

Her breathing was coming in small pants, interrupting his thoughts and drawing his gaze back to her chest. The perfect handful. The right size to cup in a palm and squeeze, feeling the nipple harden in the palm of his hand.

Her nipples did harden—under his gaze.

"Well, I'm afraid to believe it."

He tore his gaze from her chest to her face. Her expression reflected the fear she spoke of and the arousal that she did not. The arousal he understood. The sexy glazed look told him she'd let him touch her now—one touch, the feather-light flick of his thumb across her lips or her nipples, the curve of his hand behind her neck as he brought her head to his, touched his lips to hers—that's all it would take for him to set the pace that would end with her tight little ass under him. The fear—well, he understood the fear of giving in to desire. Shy women, embarrassed by their response to a man's gyrating hips or his near-nakedness, were common in his business.

But she didn't seem shy. "Why?" he demanded in a low voice.

"Because I'd be believing a lie."

He wasn't lying, but . . . "If you believe it, what does it matter?" He held the photo up and flipped it around so that the image faced her. "I satisfied her need, made the illusion seem real. That's what she wanted. The fantasy."

"Having—*enjoying*—the fantasy, all the while knowing it's a lie, would be worse than not having it at all."

A real smile tugged at his lips. What was she? Twenty-seven? Twenty-eight? She suddenly seemed much younger and idealistic. Once upon a time, he'd felt that way. His urge to smile disappeared. "Really?"

She nodded.

A blast of endorphins hit his brain, catching him off guard. Sexual interest mingled with desire—the urge to prove her wrong. It'd been years since anything—anyone—had incited that desire.

Congratulations. You're still alive. Now, say goodbye and get to work.

Instead, Johnny stared at her, noticing her skin was still flushed, though he suspected it was due to conviction, not embarrassment. But arousal seemed to show in the stiff way she held herself, leaning back slightly as if afraid to touch him.

Excitement fluttered through him, ignited by her desire and by his body's response, but it was the challenge that set off the biggest flash. Not the dime-a-dozen challenge of seducing a woman so that giving in felt like the decision had been taken out of her hands and, therefore, was acceptable. But rather, the successful seduction of a woman who was afraid of being seduced because she didn't believe in the power of fantasy.

Yeah, like fantasy's working so well for you. Maybe you *want it to be real.*

Now, there was a dumbass thought.

Johnny moved to his desk drawer. "If I dance for you and can't make you enjoy the fantasy . . ."

Reaching into his back pocket, he withdrew his keys and unlocked the drawer. ". . . all the while knowing it's a lie . . ."

Taking out his checkbook and a pen, he wrote a check. ". . . and yet feel it's *better* than not having it at all . . ."

He paused and turned back toward her. He tore the check from the pad and placed it on the desk, pushing it with his fingertip to the corner nearest her. "Then this is yours."

3

Tina took the check, staring at it in disbelief, not sure if she was more shocked by the fact that he was offering her money or the amount of money itself.

"That's the going rate for my top guys."

Twenty-five hundred dollars? Not only did that seem like a lot of money for dancing, it seemed like a lot of money to bet.

A part of her was tempted—but not by the check. She'd wanted to believe that the heat that'd been burning in his eyes and the sexiness in the curve of his lips was because he'd been attracted to her.

Because no man had ever looked at her like that. Not even David. When David had looked at her, he'd seemed to ignore her birthmark and she, being a naïve seventeen-year-old, had mistaken what she'd thought was acceptance for desire. And been proven wrong on both.

But *this* man . . .

He'd run his gaze over her face, her *whole* face,

taking in the mishmash of color that marred her skin, letting his eyes linger there, tracing its swirls and circles of imperfection, then gazing into her eyes— *both* of them—with heat simmering in his.

And it had been wonderful, to feel wanted and, for one long second . . . beautiful. She'd loved the feeling and reveled in its uniqueness.

Then rational thought had intervened, reminding her that he was the consummate actor and he had only been proving a point.

So what? You loved the feeling.

Oh God, she *had*. It had been the most amazing thing she'd ever felt. But she'd meant what she'd said, because having her heart's desire acted out by someone who didn't mean it came at a steep price. David had proven that the one time they'd had sex— her first and last time—the night Brianna had been conceived.

But you didn't know David was acting. You know Johnny is.

True. With David, she'd felt betrayed by the lie. But with Johnny, there was no lie to be betrayed by.

Would it *really* be so bad to give in and let go, and experience, through fantasy, the feelings she craved most but would never, ever have in real life? Could the once-in-a-lifetime experience of the fantasy *really* be better than not having the experience at all?

Plus, it was only a dance. It wasn't like she'd be doing anything that would cause irreparable damage.

Shaken and confused by her traitorous thoughts, Tina returned her attention to the present. She desperately searched for something mundane to focus on, choosing the check. She stared at it, surprised to see his name—Johnny Guerra—instead of a company name, at the top.

'Johnny' sounded easy-going and approachable, which he was not.

'Guerra' sounded strong and masculine, which he was.

She held it out to him. "Money isn't everything to everyone."

He took it. "It is to me."

Another surprise. She hadn't been expecting that. Had something happened to him to make all enjoyment in life revolve around money?

For her, money had always been a means to an end, never *the* end. Things didn't make her happy. It was life's little moments that did: Her daughter Brianna's laugh. The shock of vibrant color in spring when the nasturtium and lobelia first bloomed. And now, try as she might, she couldn't ignore it: Johnny's beautiful face, close enough that if she took one small step forward she could stand on tiptoe and reach his lips. She could trace them with her tongue, tasting the spiciness of his flesh, before pressing her mouth against his and closing her eyes. Before leaning against him and . . .

She looked away from his tempting lips. "I think there's so much more to life."

Tina cringed at the soft, dreamy quality to her tone, as if she were six years old and talking of unicorns and castles and princes. The warmth flooded her face, making her want to turn away.

"So you think I'm missing out on life?"

But she couldn't turn away. The humor in his tone kept her in place. The seemingly natural half-smile held her spellbound. The sparkle of amusement in his eyes mesmerized her.

She'd thought him beautiful before, but he was deadly gorgeous like this, when he seemed to drop the veneer of control, to just *be*.

"I think . . ."

She didn't know what she thought. She couldn't think. She felt as if she was on the world's steepest free-fall roller coaster, perched at the top. Her stomach felt lodged in her chest, her lungs felt blocked, unable to take in air. The blood thundered in her ears.

He took the tiny step forward that she'd fantasized about taking.

Without thinking, she took a step backward, suddenly fearing what she'd imagined.

His finger touched her lip, scrambling her last coherent thought. "You don't want to believe I could be attracted to you because it *might* be a lie."

He traced her upper lip, his light touch leaving a trail of sensation that sent a shiver through her body and a jolt of awe through her mind at the realization that such a simple caress could cause such delicious turmoil.

"Then, when I assure you I'm not lying, you're *afraid* to believe it."

He traced her lower lip.

Her lips parted and her breath escaped in a harsh whisper, as if it had been trapped inside forever, waiting for that exact moment of freedom.

"And then I offered you a dance of your choosing . . ." He lowered his lids and his expression turned slumberous. ". . . to show you the *pleasure* of a fantasy . . ."

'Pleasure' hung in the air, bringing images of his strong fingers leaving her lips to explore her body, strumming her most sensitive spots until she thrashed and trembled, moaning and pleading.

With his other hand, he waved the check resting between his fore- and middle fingers—the same fingers she'd imagined stroking her body. "You decline by giving this back without countering with something you do want."

Oh, with the images of 'pleasure' still floating through her mind and sending waves of need coiling through her body, Tina could think of a dozen things she wanted.

"That's an awful lot of hiding for someone who embraces life. Are you sure *I'm* the one missing out on life?"

He dropped his hand.

Tina took a couple of deep, though silent, breaths, hoping the oxygen would spread calmness through her system. She felt shaky and dazed. She struggled to regain control of her body—and her mind— preparing herself to meet his gaze and the cocky knowingness of how he'd affected her shining there.

She raised her eyes to his.

And her shaky calm dissolved.

His irises had darkened to a chocolaty brown, but not with heat or challenge, though a glimmer of the latter was still there. The look he gave her seemed . . . softer. As if he'd asked her a genuine question and was waiting for the answer.

The question. What had been the question?

Tina blinked, trying to focus.

Something about missing out.

That's a lot of hiding . . . Are you sure I'm *the one missing out on life?*

Oh. Right. The implication that she was hiding and

missing out on life.

After David, she'd withdrawn, shut down, swearing off stupid ideals of love and romance and men. After Brianna, she'd withdrawn further, limiting her world to her mother, her daughter, and her business, even changing her hours to the night shift to further reduce contact with people.

With men.

By limiting the scope of her world, she limited her needs and wants—except on those nights when they refused to stay bottled up inside—focusing on those that were necessary and attainable, while keeping her emotional world controlled, safe, and . . . numb.

So, yes, she guessed she had been hiding and missing out on life.

Until she'd started looking at his photos and wondering.

Until tonight, when he'd ignited the needs and wants she tried so desperately to bury.

Until now, when he'd made her realize she had been living but not alive.

Because at that moment, Tina felt alive in a way she never had before—literally alive, as if every cell and nerve had suddenly turned on and sent need roiling through her—the sensual need, the need to feel like a woman, not just a mother. The need to act, to go after all that . . . *feeling*—everything that he'd made her feel since the moment he entered the room. Everything that she'd missed out on but convinced herself she didn't need and could never have, but, against her will, still yearned for. Yearning that was so strong it was like a physical ache that filled her body. Yearning that stole her nights, keeping her awake with a hunger to touch and be touched, desire and be desired, feel beautiful and see beauty.

She'd been able to resist the pull, the desire, the need until encountering this Johnny—the Johnny staring down at her with the soft eyes and the soft lips, tempting her even more than the knowing and cocky Johnny. Because this Johnny felt different. He didn't seem to be turning on the charm. He didn't seem to be trying to seduce for the sake of seducing. His actions felt natural. They felt . . . real. Even though he might be acting.

What does it matter? I satisfied her need, made the fantasy seem real. That's what she wanted. The fantasy.

She remembered the words he'd spoken towards the beginning of it all.

Did it matter?

Regardless of whether he was acting or being real, he had made her lose herself in the moment and feel in ways she never had before. And, heaven help her, she wanted more. More of the reality, or fantasy, or whatever it was, that she'd given up on ever having in real life, for just a little bit longer.

Having—enjoying—*the fantasy, all the while knowing it's a lie, would be worse than not having it at all.*

Her words, spoken with the naiveté of ignorance, before she knew the allure of fantasy. Her words, spoken with the conviction based on David's lies.

But this was nothing like David.

David had lied and played a mean game, promising her love.

Johnny was being honest, promising her nothing but a simple, short fantasy.

David had promised her forever.

Johnny was promising her minutes.

She had gotten over the pain of David's betrayal.

But she had not gotten over the pain of her unfulfilled desires.

Her gaze went back to the check.

You decline by giving this back without countering with something you do want.

But, oh, how very, very much she wanted . . .

She looked at Johnny.

He raised a brow. The corner of his mouth quirked. His eyes were still warm and liquid like melted chocolate.

She snapped her eyes closed, momentarily hiding from the tempting man inches away from her. The man who sent her blood rushing from her brain to her breasts, spreading warmth that brought her nipples to life, before winding lower and weaving a path of tingles along her skin.

Taking a deep breath and willing the blood back to her brain where it was needed, she opened her eyes. "Okay."

Surprise flickered through his. "Okay?"

You're playing with fire.

She was tired of playing it safe. Of hiding.

She nodded.

His lips curved into a smile that said he'd already won.

You're going to get hurt.

No. "Going to get hurt" implied the pain of betrayal. Yes, she was going *to hurt*. After getting her heart's desire wrapped up in the fantasy, when the fantasy ended, yes, it was going to hurt. But the pain after would be worth the ecstasy of before.

If she made the pain worth her while. And to make opening herself up to needs and wants that had lain dormant worthwhile, she wanted more than a few minutes of fantasy.

She took the check from his hand and ripped it in half. "I don't want your money. When *I* win, I want to give you a second chance."

"A second chance." His tone was amused.

"Yeah. To apply your award-winning acting skills to a . . ." She licked her lip, suddenly nervous of saying what she really wanted. More time. A longer fantasy that she could replay and relive forever after.

His gaze dropped to her mouth, then back to her eyes. The warm chocolate in his eyes had been replaced by liquid smoke, giving her the courage to go on.

She cleared her throat. " . . . romantic date with me. The fantasy of one, of course." There, she'd said it, sounding casual and confident, as if indifferent to his reaction.

"Of course." His words seemed slightly sarcastic. His expression seemed to say, *sure, whatever*, still confident of her loss. "And for me to lose, what is this dance that you're convinced I can't perform?"

At that, Tina's confidence returned as her mind conjured up the one thing in the world that he, regardless of how talented an actor he was, would never, ever be able to fake and make her believe. "A dance that conveys you're my husband. My doting, attentive, loving husband."

His smile disappeared.

You're going to regret this.

"My doting, attentive, loving husband who has just discovered that he's going to be a father for the first time."

His face seemed to pale. He opened his mouth, then closed it.

For the first time since she'd met him, Johnny seemed speechless and nonplussed.

4

Johnny was vaguely aware of her soft gasp. A gasp he might have been able to appreciate, to let echo through his body and stroke his nerve endings to arousal. If not for those two words ringing in his ears, drowning out all other sound.

For a moment, he'd been in the present, a willing participant, aware of the woman in front of him. Surprisingly, not sexually—well, not *just* sexually. Amused by the childlike wonder in her voice as she mused about life, shocked by the way she'd trembled from the mere touch of his fingers against her lips, amazed by the jolt her shiver sent through his body, surprised by what looked like embarrassment that had flashed through her eyes as she'd asked for a simple fantasy date.

But what had shocked him the most was that, for that one moment, without thinking about it or trying to avoid it, he'd been interested and engaged in the present.

Until those two words yanked him into the past.

Husband. Father.

Two innocent words that Johnny read or heard daily, words his men used to announce events in their lives that he congratulated them on but would never apply to himself.

You did, once.

From nowhere, the image hit him. A woman's silky black hair resting against the beige examining chair as she stared at the ultrasound monitor, gazing at the little nubs, barely recognizable as little hands and fingers, feet and toes, of her son.

His son. Their son.

Johnny's stomach hitched in a way that had nothing to do with lust. His blood swooshed through his veins, echoing in his ears, bringing a rush of dizziness that had nothing to do with arousal. A bolt of pain shot through his heart.

"Scared?"

He didn't answer. At that moment, he couldn't summon a smartass reply.

Instead, he took a shaky breath and willed himself to relax. The flashbacks were coming more frequently. For a while there he'd been able to make it through weeks, months—even show up at weddings or christenings when he was invited, or give hip-hop dance lessons to boys at the local Y—like normal. But the images were coming almost weekly now. Wham! Out of nowhere, with no recognizable trigger, he'd see . . . them. Marta and his unborn son.

Only it wasn't mere seeing. It was feeling and experiencing, as if he were reliving a moment instead of simply remembering it. It was always some happy moment, never The Day or what had led up to it, which almost made it worse. Because of him, there hadn't been many happy moments. Because of him, there never would be again.

You need to deal with this shit, J, Brandon had said, after one of Johnny's episodes.

Yeah, like you're dealing with yours? Johnny had shot back.

And that had been that.

"Well, the words 'husband' and 'father' scare a lot of men."

Johnny turned his attention outward, once again focusing on the woman in front of him, watching a glittery hardness flicker through her eyes before the amusement returned, noticing the curve of her lips tighten slightly before her smile relaxed them.

Focus on her.

That's what he did. Focused on others.

My dance request is that you are my husband . . . My doting, attentive, loving husband who has just discovered he's going to be a father for the first time.

Husband. Father.

That was *her* request. Those were *her* words.

Something was going on with *her*. Women came to Hot Dreams to get away from real life. They asked for sexy firefighters or cops, not husbands.

This is about her. Not me.

His stomach began to relax. His pulse started to slow. He took one last deep breath, cleansing away the painful memories.

Her expression—the glimmer in her eyes, the curl of her lips—taunted him. Her fleeting discomfort was hidden behind her look of challenge. "I understand if *even you* can't do it."

His sudden panic was now buried in his psyche.

This is about her.

He pushed the last remnant of pain away and eased into Hot Dreams mode. Ten years ago, in his first and last session with a shrink, she'd told him to try guided meditation to help turn off his 'anxiety and obsessive thoughts of self-blame' and overcome his depression. He'd snorted, told her imagining himself on a beach wasn't going to solve a damn thing, and walked out.

But easing into Hot Dreams mode was something like guided meditation. Except, instead of imagining mounds of sand, he imagined the pillowy mounds of breasts. Instead of feeling imaginary gusts of ocean breeze against his skin, the jerky sighs of feminine arousal caressed his eardrums. These images and more would fill his mind, crowding out other thought, sparking ripples of lust through his body that were converted to energy, readying him for action.

Hot Dreams mode didn't solve his problems, but it certainly helped him avoid them. Or rather, it had.

He let her breasts, cocooned in the snug t-shirt, and the gasps she'd made earlier overwhelm his senses.

Easing back into his true self, he said. "Oh, I can do it. And here's what *I* want when *I* win."

He let his eyes travel over her body—from the white-tipped toenails to the curve of her hips, over her flat stomach, lingering on her breasts, returning to her face, noting the smile was completely gone and that her lips parted under his gaze, her pink tongue darting out to add moisture that he wanted to take, to share, to taste. He returned his eyes to hers, noticing they had darkened.

He smiled. "I want to show you the real Johnny." *His* version of the real Johnny.

~~~~

At his look, as he traced her body with his eyes, seeming to caress her flesh wherever his gaze rested, Tina's stomach dropped to the tip of her toes then rushed back to her abdomen like a live yo-yo, taking the blood with it, then bringing it back in a rush, leaving her lightheaded.

At his words, her breath froze in her throat.

His look and his words were blatantly sexual, meant to rattle her.

They worked. She was rattled.

He took a step back and held his arm out in an after-you motion. "Shall we begin?"

She was doubly rattled. "What?"

He raised a brow.

"Now?"

"Scared?" His voice taunted, throwing her word back at her.

"No."

Liar.

She wasn't scared. She was . . . startled.

Liar.

A little surprised.

Liar.

Okay, she was a little scared. Not of losing—there was no chance of that. But rather . . . everything had happened so fast. From innocently ogling his photos to meeting him. From being against fantasies to wanting one. From being emotionally and physically numb to being on fire. To wanting no man to wanting him. From feeling invisible to feeling desired.

It was too much. She needed to process everything that had happened, regroup, and regain control. She looked at her watch. "Oh, I have another client."

His lips twitched. "You will have plenty of time to get to your client. One song. One dance. You'll be out of here in less than six minutes."

"Oh."

Once again, she scrambled to regain her wits. Would she ever feel normal around this man?

I hope not.

Well, right then she wanted a little normalcy, wishing for the control she'd felt just minutes before when he'd been shocked. That shock, which she'd thoroughly enjoyed, was long gone. Oh, but the look on his face when she'd requested a husband and father. His eyes had widened ever so slightly and his jaw had dropped, though not enough to part his lips. It was as if she'd asked him to do a sexy dance as Hannibal Lecter from *Silence of the Lambs*. While she hadn't expected such an extreme reaction, she'd felt a frisson of pleasure at getting it, thrilled to have discomfited him by asking for something that perhaps no other woman had.

Now, *she* was uncomfortable.

But he was right. It was only six minutes. Processing and regrouping could wait a handful of minutes. And she could certainly maintain a semblance of control for that long.

Squaring her shoulders, she walked past him, feeling relieved that he hadn't crowded her, forcing her to brush against him in passing. She paused outside the door, waiting for him to join her, and then followed past the areca palms she'd been so proud of, then the man cave—the lounge area with the pool table, which Tina had admired her first night, remembering the many nights she'd played pool—and won—to raise the money to start Plants Alive.

They entered a room she'd only glanced inside before, since there were no plants to water. The room reminded her of the one where Brianna took ballet lessons, only no bars lined the walls. Instead, windows that looked out over the twinkling city lights of downtown Seattle took up the wall in front of her. The wall to the right and opposite the windows had floor-to-ceiling mirrors. The one to the left was bare.

"Do you dance here?"

He walked to a Bose docking station sitting on the window ledge. Tina couldn't help but notice the way his slacks hugged his ass, draping the round cheeks before falling in a perfect crease down the length of his legs.

"My guys practice for competitions and shows here."

"You don't practice with them?"

"I don't dance anymore."

Then why was he dancing now? She filed that away in the Process Later file.

Music filled the room, taking her by surprise. She'd expected something fast, with a frenetic beat and throbbing bass. Instead, slow notes and soft lyrics teased her ears from the speakers in the ceiling. Whereas the former would scream sex, the heartfelt crooning of the male vocalist singing about love created a mood of . . . yearning.

A flicker of unease rippled through her.

"Stand here."

She walked toward to the front of the room and stopped near him, facing the window.

"Face the mirror."

"I don't . . . like mirrors."

He placed his hands on her shoulders and turned

her around. She looked at him behind her, in the mirror. "You won't be looking at yourself."

"Oh. Right."

Johnny moved away. She continued watching his reflection, hypnotized.

He began unbuttoning his shirt. His movements were functional, going through motions he went through each day, with no apparent intent to arouse. But as his fingers moved from one pearly circle to the next, Tina found the movements seductive. She imagined what it would feel like for him to unbutton her shirt, if she'd had buttons. The pads of his fingers skimming her skin, the back of his knuckles brushing the swell of her breasts.

She looked for a distraction, striving for normalcy. "I thought stripping was part of your routine."

"I tailor my routine to my audience." He turned his head in her direction as he undid the last button. "And you watching me strip is not what this is about, is it?" His voice was soft, seductive. His eyes were dark. He slid the shirt from his shoulders and tossed it aside.

Tina gasped.

Because of his words, since he was right.

Because of his body, since he was hot.

His chest was even more beautiful than in his photos, with just enough muscle to exude strength and good health, instead of steroids and half-days spent in the gym. It was defined and sculpted, reminding her of a marble statue of a male torso in the Louvre that had appeared on a postcard her friend Sarah had sent her from France.

Johnny drew a slim remote from the ledge, held it toward the iPod and flicked a button. The song started over from the beginning.

As the light strains from the guitar and the swish of the brush against the drum filled the room, he came to her and stopped behind her. He moved his legs, first one, then shifted his weight, then the other. His shoulders rocked to one side, paused, then rocked to the other. Slow and smooth. His head rocked slightly, following the slow rhythm set by his legs, matched by the rolling sway of his shoulders.

Only his pant legs, brushing against her jeans in synch with the drum, touched her. Only the heat of his body caressed her.

Somehow, feeling the heat of him but not him, seeing part of him behind her but not all of him, was even more erotic. Because it made her imagine what his touch would feel like, and made her wonder if she would feel it and when.

Which made her crave it.

He picked up a lock of her hair and tucked it behind her ear, still without touching her skin, making her want to tilt her head into his touch.

As the male voice, soft and intimate, crooned about some woman being his angel, Johnny raised his eyes to hers.

His eyes were dark and intense and filled with lust. The kind of look she'd seen on a guy's face in movies during some hot love scene—when she'd been a teenager and still watched those movies—right before he ripped the clothes off of the lead woman.

Only, she wasn't watching a movie. She was watching him.

And he wasn't looking at an actress. He was looking at her.

Tina inhaled sharply.

His body swayed. His head rocked from side to side, the movement slight. But his gaze didn't waver.

No one had ever looked at her like that. Yeah, she'd said that about the look he'd given her in the office. But this was more intense because he didn't look away. There were no distractions. There was no conversation.

No *verbal* conversation.

But his eyes said she was the only woman in his world. The world had stopped at this moment, this room, narrowing to just him and how he made her feel.

Irresistible. Wanted. Gorgeous.

It's not real. He's acting.

Yes, her mind knew that. But her body and, at that moment, her heart didn't care.

Johnny raised a hand. She watched his forefinger stop less than an inch in front of her lips and trace them before moving down, under her chin, following the valley between her breasts, which were rising and falling rapidly.

Tina forced her breathing to slow and appear normal.

Johnny raised his other hand, stopping in front of her chest. Both hands were slightly cupped, as if seconds away from caressing her breasts.

Tina felt—and saw—her nipples harden, as if trying to reach out to him. Heat rushed to her cheeks. It should have been embarrassment, but she knew it wasn't.

His hands moved lower, their movement in synch with his body, stopping mere inches away from her stomach.

Oh, how she wanted to grab his hands and press

them against her, to lean back and press her ass against his groin and move it against him, perhaps get a gasp out of him, for a change.

Before she could lose herself in what that would be like, he was in front of her, reaching for her hands and placing them on his shoulders.

Such a simple act.

And yet it sent tremors through Tina.

She hadn't felt a man's naked flesh under her fingertips since David. And David had been a boy, all sharp angles and bony edges, who'd felt nothing like this. Johnny's skin felt smooth as marble. Strength rippled under his muscles, tensing and relaxing them. She willed her fingers to remain relaxed, lightly resting on him, instead of running them along his shoulders, then down to his forearms, tracing and squeezing, before moving upward, slipping up his neck and into his hair.

While she struggled not to caress him, he made no effort to touch her.

While she fought to remain still, to prevent the sway of her body toward his, he made no effort to close the distance between them. Her hands on him were the only physical connection.

Her gaze dropped to his chest, taking in his pecs, his tiny pebbled nipples, before moving down to his stomach, watching muscles flex and relax with each movement. His hands circled the air near her hips, miming holding her. His hips pressed forward, then back, in sync with his chest and abs, as they moved in the wavy S-like motion of a belly dancer.

Slow and smooth.

Sexy and hot.

Her gaze dropped even lower, taking in the bulge

at the front of his slacks, causing a noticeable tent from his hard—

He was hard.

Tina gasped. Even he couldn't fake that.

But it's not you *he's reacting to.*

Maybe not, but she was going to enjoy the result, was going to pretend it was her.

You're losing.

Losing. Winning. The words seemed to be a meaningless string of vowels and consonants.

Until his hands moved to the front, stopping about four inches in front of her stomach, making slow circular rubbing motions.

With that, Tina remembered what she'd asked for, what this dance was all about.

My dance request is that you are my husband . . . My doting, attentive, loving husband who has just discovered he's going to be a father for the first time.

With that, the air began to leak from her arousal bubble, turning her attention from what he made her feel to what he was doing.

His hips undulated and gyrated as he lowered his body, stopping when his knees reached the floor and his head was even with her stomach.

His hands were still in front of her stomach, air-caressing it slowly in time to the music. His gaze was directed at her stomach, seemingly watching his hands.

Unexpectedly, Tina tensed.

The singer proclaimed she was his angel.

Johnny caressed.

Suddenly, her heart raced and adrenaline surged through her as she stared down at him, at the cupped fingers making small circles in the air, at his long dark eyelashes hiding his eyes. Whereas before she'd resisted the urge to pull him toward her, now she struggled not to push him away.

Johnny dropped his hands and moved his head forward, toward her. He pursed his lips slightly, planting an air kiss on her imaginary baby growing inside her stomach.

Just as she'd once imagined Brianna's father doing.

The soft swish of the brush caressed the drums.

His lips again brushed her "pregnant" belly.

Tina resisted the urge to step back.

With each soft swish of the brush against the drums, his lips brushed her "stomach."

With each soft swish of the brush against the drums, Tina's body felt stiffer, her throat felt tighter.

Johnny was not her husband, lovingly caressing the mound of their unborn child, just as David had never been. Out of nowhere, a moan filled with loss—for the husband she'd thought David would be, for the happy father she thought her unborn child would have, for the woman she could have been— rumbled in the back of her throat, as if the loss she had dealt with and gotten over was happening today instead of ten years ago.

Johnny looked up and his gaze caught hers.

She saw lust there, but it was fading, warming, turning into something different.

Without warning, fullness formed at the back of her eyes. As tears pooled in her eyes, Johnny's expression changed. Softness wiped out lust, growing ever warmer, infinitely more caring, until it resembled . . . love.

The love she'd expected to see the night Brianna was conceived, when she'd given herself to David as proof of her love for him.

The love she'd felt for him as she'd held his body against hers and watched him, his eyes closed, as he pumped his hips, moving in and out of her.

The love that had turned out to be an illusion—a lie—when he'd opened his eyes and looked at her with indifference, instead.

And then he'd left. Withdrew his body from hers, got dressed, ignored her pleas, and left.

Pain clenched her chest.

Confusion flickered through Johnny's gaze.

Her body trembled.

Johnny's confusion morphed into a glimmer of something like ... anger. Just like the anger in Sam's—David's best friend's—eyes.

As Johnny began to rise, he said, "Wh—"

But instead of Johnny, Tina heard Sam's laughing voice say, "Why? Because he never loved you. He fucked you to win a fifty-dollar bet, Freak."

Tears ran down her cheeks.

Tina yanked her hands from Johnny's shoulders as if they suddenly burned her. Turning on her toes, she ran to the door, nearly knocking down the guy in the doorway as she raced by.

5

Johnny stayed where he was, knees still pressed to the floor, hands now resting on his thighs. He stared at nothing, all focus inward, as his mind tried to wrap itself around what the hell had just happened. The heat from her body still swirled in front of him, tempting him to reach out and touch her and pull her against him. He still felt the swollen stomach inches from his face, a stomach that had seemed more real than the real one—Marta's.

His lips still tingled as if he'd brushed them across real skin instead of thin air, skin smooth and tight as it covered his child, skin that he'd barely touched when Marta had been carrying Junior. Not because he had any aversion to doing so, more because it hadn't occurred to him. He'd been too busy stressing over how, at eighteen, he was going to support a kid and a wife he hadn't planned on.

As he'd danced, regret had stabbed his stomach that he hadn't felt his son growing when he'd had the chance.

Longing had jolted his body. Longing to feel what he would never be able to feel. Longing to see the son that he would never be able to see. Longing to save the wife whom he'd never loved and who had never loved him.

Pain had stabbed his gut, taking his breath, and then he'd looked up and seen pain in her eyes reflected back at him, pain that he had somehow caused.

Just like with Marta.

Anger had flooded him. Anger at himself because, once again, he'd caused another undeserving woman pain.

What the hell just happened?

Where the fuck had all that shit come from? He raked a hand through his hair, surprised to find it was shaking.

Fuck.

"Who was that?"

Johnny whipped his head to the doorway where Brandon stood.

Shit.

He stood, stunned to feel the trembling in his quads, as if he'd just done ten reps of leg squats with two hundred-pound barbells.

What the hell!

"Well?"

"What?" Johnny walked toward the window, striving to shake out the tremor in his legs. He grabbed the remote and stopped the song in mid-note, hoping to erase from the room the last reminder of what should have been a simple dance.

Only it wasn't that simple. His mind wouldn't shut down.

"Who was that?"

He didn't even know her name. He hadn't asked. Names hadn't seemed important at the time. "The gardener."

But now, her name seemed immensely important. He'd get it from the property management office. He needed to know who she was.

"The gardener?"

He wanted to know why she had affected him like this.

"I hate to tell you this but we don't have a garden."

He wanted to know what the hell had happened.

"She's the . . . the . . ." Johnny waved a hand in irritation at Brandon's persistence. "The plant waterer."

He wanted to know what had been going on in her mind, what had gone wrong, what he had done to send her running away. Even though it bothered the hell out of him that he gave a flying fuck about her mind and was even still thinking about her. Out of sight, out of mind. One of his favorite mottos. One that he lived up to.

Until now.

"Is that like the Dog Whisperer?"

The amusement in Brandon's voice barely registered.

"So you—He Who Does Not Dance—*you* were dancing for the plant waterer?"

"It wasn't a dance. It was a bet."

A simple bet. A simple interaction that had become hellaciously complicated. He did not do complicated. And yet, here he was.

"Is there a point where this conversation is going

to start making sense?"

"No." Because there was no making sense of it.

One minute, things had been proceeding exactly as planned. He'd been into it, instantly hard at the sight of her nipples as they'd turned into small marbles merely from his gaze. She'd been into it, too. Her eyes had had that soft I-love-what-you're-doing-to-me look that he totally got off on. And then she'd dropped her gaze to his cock and her gaze had turned awestruck and filled with wonder, almost . . . amazed, as if shocked that she had caused that.

The naturalness of it, the rawness of it, unhidden and uncontrived, had made him feel like he was back in junior high, two seconds from creaming his swim trunks when he'd caught a glimpse of Susie Jamison's breasts spilling out of her skimpy bikini top.

Only, he hadn't been looking at the gardener's breasts, he'd been looking at her eyes, feeding off of that look, until the mood had darkened and the light had gone out of her eyes.

And then the shit—unlike his usual episodic shit—had hit him.

And then, like a wounded deer, she'd run away.

Which should have filled him with relief, like it would any other time. She was gone. Game over. Out of sight, out of mind.

Only it didn't, which led him to the thing that rocked him the most out of everything that had happened: He'd wanted to run after her.

What. The. Fuck.

He jerked his shirt off the floor and put it back on, then turned to Brandon, suddenly glad for the distraction. "What are you doing here?"

"I figured you'd be here. I wanted to know what

you thought about Club Boudoir."

Johnny looked at his watch. The dance had lasted less than five minutes and yet it was the most intense dance of his career. An image of tear-filled eyes appeared. He pushed it away. "You came down here at 10:23 PM to ask me about a club?"

"Yep. I'm trying to be more *focused* on work, like you said."

"I said you should be focused *at* work." He tucked his shirt in and picked up his tie. With relief, he noticed his hand was no longer shaking. "I also said you should focus on your marriage when not at work. Where's Christie?"

Brandon shrugged as if his wife's location was of no importance.

Johnny knew better.

"Speaking of women, the gardener's a first. A woman running like hell from you." Brandon laughed and shook his head. "Not to mention she did *not* look like your type."

The image of her face, its profusion of unexpected pinks in various hues separated by ribbons of honey-colored creaminess, flashed in front of him. He whirled around to Brandon. "What the hell is that supposed to mean?"

Surprise flickered over Brandon's face before curiosity replaced it. "Well, now. *That's* interesting."

Warmth tinted Johnny's cheeks, causing him to turn away.

"I meant she seems *nice*."

Considering Brandon had seen her for a couple of minutes max and hadn't interacted with her, his conclusion shouldn't have made sense. But Johnny knew what he meant. Jeans that hugged her ass perfectly but had no designer label. A simple t-shirt, slightly faded from numerous washings. Glossy hair, highlighted by nature, with a simple honey-lemony scent that came from a shampoo bottle, not chemicals mixed to create a perfume sold in a fancy salon with a celebrity name.

Nice. No artifice. Most definitely not his type.

"What's going on, J?" Brandon's voice was finally serious.

"Nothing." She was just another woman that he'd met, flirted with and, despite things not going as expected, would never see again.

"Nothing at all." The words went well beyond the fantasy that encompassed his life, slipping into the realm of a lie, though he didn't know why. While he wanted to believe she was just another woman, same as any other, she wasn't. While he hated wanting to see her again, he did.

He vowed he would not see her again, all the while knowing he would. "Since you're here, let's talk about Club Boudoir."

6

Tina stood at the sink, rinsing orange juice off her hands while staring sightlessly out the window overlooking the back yard. Her mind was miles away, replaying the dance in Johnny's office for the thousandth time.

A week later, she still couldn't believe what had happened, couldn't believe she'd run from the room—and as if that wasn't bad enough—*crying*, for heaven's sake.

And she still didn't know why.

It wasn't because she was still in pain about David. In fact, she rarely thought of him. When she did, she might wish he—and that night—had never happened so she wouldn't have had to spend years rebuilding her self-esteem or obsessively asking herself *how could he* and *why* or berating herself for being so incredibly young and foolish, so hungry for acceptance and love, that she'd ignored the warning signs.

But then, she reminded herself, if that hadn't happened, she also wouldn't have Brianna—and while she could imagine a life with all of those other things, she could not imagine a life without her nine-year-old daughter.

So she simply didn't think about David or the past or what might have been. But on those few times she did, when the sadness, remorse or whatever else surfaced, she'd never felt like crying.

She really hadn't thought that a husband/proud father dance would be a big deal, other than a surefire way to win and prove Johnny wrong.

Which made last Friday triply humiliating. Of all the times to experience all that emotion, why in the middle of the most fantastic dance of her life? A dance she still couldn't stop thinking about and a man she couldn't stop wanting.

Well, on the bright side, you won—and with such drama.

At that thought, Tina snorted. Like she'd really be able to collect on that after coming across like a nutcase.

"Hi, Mom."

She turned as Brianna walked toward her. "Oh, hi, hon. I didn't hear you come in."

"What's so funny?"

"Nothing. Just something that happened at work."

Brianna wrinkled her nose. "What could be funny at your work? Did a spider plant tell a joke?"

Tina ruffled Brianna's hair. "Ha ha. Want some orange juice?"

"Sure. Do we have granola bars?"

"Yep." Tina grabbed a bar, poured Brianna some juice, and set both on the table.

Brianna sat down.

"How was school?"

"Okay, I guess. Jenny's new stepdad dropped her

off today."

"Oh? I didn't realize Jenny's mom had remarried."

"Yeah. She married Jenny's uncle."

"What!"

Brianna shrugged, digging through her backpack. "Jenny said he was her uncle—even though her real dad didn't know him—before they got married and now she's supposed to call him Dad."

Tina smothered a laugh.

"How can he change from uncle to dad?"

"Um, well, sometimes they're just called uncles . . . " Oh, Lord, how was she going to explain this?

Brianna frowned. "Why?" She took out her iPad.

Tina latched on to that with relief. "Hey, no iPad before homework. You know the rules."

"I did it all at school. Guess what?" Her face brightened, *faux* uncles and newly appointed stepdads forgotten. "There's going to be a talent competition at school with prizes and everything."

"That's great!" Tina's enthusiasm sounded a bit excessive, even to her own ears.

"Yeah." Thankfully, Brianna hadn't seemed to notice. "And I'm going to enter. I'm going to dance."

At the mention of the word 'dance,' like Pavlov's dogs that were trained to salivate at the sound of a bell, Tina's mind went immediately to Johnny and the other part of that night she couldn't forget. The way his body had shimmied, making her want him. The look in his eyes that had made her feel desirable. The fact that no matter how many times she told herself not to, she still wanted him—the completion of the fantasy she'd prematurely aborted.

"But I need to think of something to do.

Something original."

Tina forced the longing from her mind and focused on Brianna. "How about that scene from *Swan Lake* you did last year in ballet?"

"Mom, I want to do something *cool.*"

"I thought that was cool."

"Moooom."

"Okay, okay."

"But I'm kinda afraid."

"Afraid of what?"

"Tammy Simmons said she's going to enter and she's going to dance, too. Only she's been taking dance lessons *her whole life.*" Brianna paused, her eyes big, brows raised, lips parted, waiting to make sure Tina understood the importance of this fact.

"I see." Though, in fact, Tina didn't. But learning from the 'cool' mistake, she was going to wait for Brianna to tell her.

"I really, *really* want to win but . . ." Brianna took a bite of her bar, then averted her gaze, suddenly interested in the fresh sunflowers in the vase on the table. "I'm not sure I'm good enough."

Tina's heart sank. "Honey, everybody—even Tammy—has doubts about themselves. That maybe they're not smart enough or thin enough . . ."

. . . or pretty enough . . .

" . . . or that people won't like them . . ."

. . . or that a man doesn't really find them attractive . . .

"So I understand why hearing about Tammy might make you doubt yourself. But thinking about what others can or cannot do is a waste of time. All you can—and should—think about is what *you* can do. And you want to win, right?"

And you want to collect your 'winnings', right?

"Yes."

Yes.

"Then you need to say to yourself, 'I'm going to win,' and then practice, work hard, and do everything you can to try to win."

Brianna looked at her with sad eyes. "But what if I don't?"

But what if he doesn't want me?

"Then you don't."

Then he doesn't.

"You live with the fact that you did the best you could, right here, right now, and you try harder next time."

Exactly!

Brianna's mouth turned down. "But I want to win this time."

But I want him now.

Tina put her arm around Brianna and hugged her. "Then put down your iPad and go dance."

Then go to Hot Dreams and get your prize.

Brianna sighed. "Okay." She slid from her chair and took her glass to the sink, then headed toward the stairs. "I love you, Mom."

"I love you, too." She smiled. "You can do this, Brianna."

You can do this, Tina.

"I'll try."

If only Tina felt brave enough to say the same thing.

7

Tina entered Johnny's office and heaved a huge sigh—of relief, of course, not disappointment—at the discovery that it was empty. She'd thought about not coming, of getting one of her staff to handle his plants. But at the last minute she remembered that she was an adult.

An adult who really wanted to see him, even if she had blown her chance at a world-altering fantasy.

She ran her hands down her skirt, smoothing the small pleats that fell away from the narrow waistline. Her simple white sundress was made from a nylon-cotton blend, dotted with small colorful flowers. The scoop neckline accented her breasts but revealed no cleavage; the form-fitting skirt accented her hips and stomach, without clinging; the hemline fell below her knees, keeping it conservative.

The dress was flattering, not sexy. She looked attractive, not obvious.

Or so she hoped.

Even though she was probably being silly, she'd

worn it for Johnny. While she couldn't undo the damage she'd done, she could at least look her best to make up for not behaving her best. She could at least maintain a good impression going forward.

She tucked her hair behind her ear. This time, she'd parted her hair on the right and swooped it over to the left, letting it hang loose to hide the only part of her birthmark she could cover—the part that traveled from her jaw, past her ear, to her temple. While she didn't delude herself that it actually hid her blemish, she felt that her hair, with its glowing color and glossy, healthy strands—which she truly felt was her best attribute—drew the eye away from her face.

She refused to cover her skin with thick, cake-like theatrical makeup like some women with birthmarks did. Using her hair was her major concession to hiding.

Well, other than avoiding people. Namely men.

Except for *this* man.

She took a deep breath, reminding herself that first and foremost, she was a professional, there to do her job like she did every day, and that secondly, while she hadn't been able to get Johnny out of her mind, he'd most likely forgotten about her and their unfortunate encounter.

If only she hadn't left the room.

She sighed, pushing aside what might have been and focusing on what was. She reached into her bag and took out the new frame and placed it on his desk with her note of apology. Next, she watered the Pothos on his bookshelf, then moved on to the Schefflera on his credenza. She reached for the plant, careful to ignore the pull of his image calling to her from the dozen filled frames.

She refused to look at a single photo, let alone touch one.

She was not going to think about him, despite the fact that he was all she'd been able to think about.

She was not going to keep wishing that things had turned out differently. That she hadn't made a fool of herself.

She was going to focus on work.

Again, she sighed, and turned toward the door.

Again, she let out a startled squeal when she saw Johnny standing there, just like last time. Only worse—or deliciously better, depending on how she looked at it. The business attire was gone and instead he wore a pair of expensive jeans, made to look worn with the denim lighter along the front of his thighs and shins, that fit him perfectly, slung low on his hips. A belt buckle peeked out below the bottom of his v-neck t-shirt, which, of course, fit his chest and arms snugly in all the right places.

A jolt of awareness so strong that it was indistinguishable from pain shot through her.

His gaze traveled over her—shoulders, breasts, waist, thighs, legs, toes—and back up. Last week in his office when he'd looked at her like that, his expression had been smoky and flirty and taunting, as if wanting her to know exactly what he was thinking. It was a look for her, meant to show her what he wanted.

Now, his look was direct, as if he wasn't just looking, but *seeing* her, stripping away the flimsy fabric covering her body and seeing the soft skin underneath. His attention was intensely focused on every part that his gaze touched, as if memorizing each curve, as if stroking every nerve. It was a look meant to satisfy him, a look that simply reflected his thoughts with no intent to prove anything to her.

And his thoughts looked deeply, darkly . . . hungry.

Tina's heart tripled its beat. She felt dizzy.

Does that mean he hasn't forgotten about Friday?

His hot gaze made it hard for her to breathe, to move, to think. She looked away, suppressing a shaky sigh of relief when she spotted the forgotten frame. She picked it up from where she'd set it on his desk and held it up. "I bought a new frame to replace the one that I broke."

He didn't even look at it. His eyes stayed locked on her face. Waiting.

For what? She didn't know what to say.

She fought the urge to fiddle with the frame or fidget under his gaze. Her mind raced, scrambling to find an impersonal, professional conversation starter, before landing on the one personal, unprofessional thing she'd promised herself she wouldn't say. "I'm sorry about last Friday."

"Which part?"

"Running away. It had nothing to do with you." This time, she did fidget a little because the rest was hard to say. But emboldened by the hunger she hoped she saw in his eyes, by the need she felt overwhelming her body, and the pep talk she'd given Brianna, she said, "I wish I had stayed."

"Doesn't matter. You won."

"What?"

He remained silent, as if her question had been hypothetical. Or more likely, he realized she was rattled, incapable of thinking, as his words echoed in her mind before finally sinking in.

Despite her embarrassing exit, he was still

interested. She could hardly believe it. It was too good to be true. But she couldn't help but wonder: *Why?*

Images of him flitted through her mind.

An image of him touching her mouth.

You don't want to believe I could be attracted to you . . .

An image of him tracing her lower lip.

I offered to show you the pleasure of fantasy . . .

An image of him moving his hips behind her, rolling his shoulders, thrusting his pelvis in time to the sultry beat.

I don't dance.

She took a deep breath, preparing to ask the second question that she shouldn't, a question that was inappropriate to the game they were playing. But being new to games, she couldn't resist. "Why are you doing . . ." *the bet, the fantasy, all of* ". . . this?"

He pushed away from the doorframe and walked toward her, stopping a few inches in front of her.

The faint scent of his cologne—a fresh citrusy smell with hints of cucumber and something woody—wafted under her nose, enveloping her neck like a lasso, making her want to lean closer, place her mouth against his neck, and . . . taste.

"Because I want to."

She gripped the frame that, until that moment, she'd forgotten she was still holding, willing herself not to step back or worse, step forward and press herself into his arms or against his body. Instead, she forced herself to appear unaffected, as if simply waiting for his answer.

He slid the frame from her hands, set it on the glass top, and sat on the edge of the desk, his gaze never leaving hers.

"Because I want you."

Tina gasped. With those words, her mind went back to the dance when she'd seen just how much he'd wanted her, when he'd been hard for her, making her wonder what it would feel like to feel him. Against her. Inside her.

"If I didn't, I wouldn't be here. If I didn't, I wouldn't be doing 'this.'" Only the meaning of 'this' had changed, no longer limited to what he had done—the looks, the innuendos, the taunts—in the past, but was being expanded to include action to be done in the future.

Right now.

He leaned forward, moving his head toward hers and at that moment Tina felt that her heart would literally stop because, *oh my God*, he was going to kiss her.

His lips met hers, the barest touch that sent waves of shock through her body. The foreignness of his caress against her sensitive flesh, unused to sensual contact, woke every nerve and muscle in her body. She moved her lips against his in wonder, loving the way her heart rate doubled with every nibble and her body weakened with every lick. When his tongue entered her mouth, exploring and tasting, Tina moaned as each swirl of his tongue sent desire flooding her body.

Johnny moved his head back, breaking off the kiss, to trail his mouth along her right jaw, nipping her earlobe before saying, "And if I didn't want you, I wouldn't be thinking about doing a lot more."

Tina shivered, from both the words and the feel of them, caressing her ear and entering her body, taking her need and desire ever higher.

A door somewhere opened. Faint masculine

laughter replaced the sound of Johnny's words still echoing in her ear.

Johnny stood and moved away, resuming his position near the door, but his eyes never left her. Heat simmered in them, as if fueled by thoughts of 'doing a lot more.'

Footfalls sounded in the hallway, moving closer.

Tina blinked. Her mind, slowed by the sensations swirling through her, finally grasped that someone was coming and Johnny was giving her time to compose herself. She took a deep breath, then exhaled. She willed her pulse to its normal, steady pace—and failed.

"Hey, J." A voice in the hallway jerked her gaze from Johnny toward the doorway, moments before a man appeared. "We're—Oh. Sorry."

Cocking her head to the left, instinctively keeping her bad side away from his direct line of sight, she recognized the guy standing in the doorway as the one she'd seen last Friday when she'd made her humiliating getaway. But what she hadn't noticed then was that he was gorgeous. Even more so than Johnny—in a more pretty-boy kind of way—but he didn't send her heart rate skyrocketing the way Johnny did.

He grinned at her. "Hi, again. I'm Brandon. And you are?"

"Tina."

"Well, Tina, we're about to play pool. Do you play?"

"Uh . . ." *Play? Play, what?*

Her brain scrambled to catch up with this change of events, to convert the need still coursing through her body, sparked by Johnny's lips, to energy needed for simple conversation.

Brandon laughed. "That's okay. He doesn't either. Unlike me, he needs all the help he can get." Still grinning, Brandon winked at Tina and left.

Oh. Right. Johnny and his friends were going to play pool.

Tina shook off her sexual daze. "Well, I will just water the Schefflera and the ferns and the palms and—" *Stop rambling on about plants!* "I'll just finish up and—"

"Stay."

One word that sounded like a request masked as a command, spoken in a clipped tone that sounded rusty as if rarely used—as if rarely used for *asking*.

One word that skipped across her skin, stroking her like fingertips, its monosyllable sending a ripple of tremors cascading through her body, leaving a trail of want and need and desire.

To stay.

"Stay." Rustiness morphed into confidence. "And 'play.'" The hint of a request dissolved into a challenge, issued as a double entendre.

Play an innocent game of pool.

Play a sinful game with him.

But . . . play in a roomful of gorgeous men.

The last one made her mouth dry—and not in anticipation. She felt out of her comfort zone with most men, but the thought of a bunch of perfect men overwhelmed and intimidated her, igniting the knee-jerk response of 'no way.'

But the first one, playing pool . . .

Pool was one thing she excelled at, the only thing that her father had left her with. He'd loved to play and she'd wanted him to love her, so she'd let him teach her and she'd practiced, convinced that if she became the best pool player, he'd stay. She had become good—raising nearly all the money to start Plants Alive by playing, money that she would have used for college if Brianna hadn't come along—but he'd still left.

The desire to make up for last Friday's humiliating retreat was a strong motivator. The old thrill of the game—one she hadn't felt since before Brianna was born—overrode her discomfort of being surrounded by hunky men whose beauty would draw attention to her unattractiveness and infused her with the confidence in her skill, skill that would command respect and diffuse her physical imperfection.

And the second one, Johnny . . .

"Well, put like that, I'll stay." *And play.*

~~~~

Tina's confidence lasted all the way to the hallway. Her sexual daze was long gone. As she stared at Johnny's back, panic flooded her body, spurring the urge to turn around and leave, uncaring that it would be the second time she'd run away, equally humiliating though for a different reason.

She always hated watching the progression of emotion that flickered across the faces of people when they saw her for the first time, which then led to discomfort over not knowing where to look, which meant staring fixedly at the right side of her face with sympathy or pity that manifested itself in exaggerated friendliness. The sympathy was the thing she hated most, because it hurt. But she never looked away, never acted like she warranted their sympathy. Despite wanting to, despite the hurt.

And those were the polite ones.

But she didn't want to experience any of that here. Being pitied by beautiful men—beautiful men who happened to be friends of Johnny's—felt . . . unbearable.

For some reason Johnny hadn't reacted. Neither had Brandon, though perhaps he had the first time he'd seen her, when she'd been too busy trying to escape to notice. But the other guys . . .

Too late now.

Johnny entered the doorway, still blocking her view.

"Finally," said a voice that was not Brandon's.

Tina took a deep breath and lifted her chin, ready to look every guy—no matter how hunky, no matter how intimidating—straight in the eye.

Johnny stepped into the room and stood to the side.

Squaring her shoulders, she entered, her attention momentarily distracted from the men around her as Johnny cupped the underside of her arm.

She'd rested her hands on his shoulders during that fateful dance and they'd just shared a soul-shaking kiss, but this was the first time he'd really touched her. Her body noticed. Tingles shot over her elbow and up her bicep, skittering across her shoulder, despite the fact that his touch was not sexual.

He took a step closer to her, his chest brushing her shoulder, his fingertips guiding and turning her, his touch and his nearness seemingly . . . possessive.

Or so she imagined.

"Tina, meet the guys. That's Darrell . . ."

"Hey." Darrell, a younger—but equally panty-melting—version of Blair Underwood, smiled and nodded in her direction.

"Nino."

"Ciao." Nino, a dead ringer for top model David Gandy in a Dolce and Gabbana ad, gave her a sexy, flirty, half-grin.

"Luke."

"Hi." Luke, looking like Brad Pitt and Paul Walker rolled into one, gave her a wink and a closed-lip smile.

"And you already met The Clown."

"Welcome, Tina. Glad you came. Our boy here needs help."

"Nice meeting you all." And Tina meant it. No one had subjected her to the usual progression of expressions. Their gazes had flickered across her face, like one did when looking at anyone, neither lingering on the profusion of colors nor ignoring them. Surprise had flickered through four sets of eyes, replaced by curiosity in a few of them, but it seemed to be over who she was and perhaps what she was doing there, not because of her appearance.

Acceptance. Normalcy.

When had she last experienced those, outside of her family and close friends? And of all places to feel it, she would never have imagined feeling it here.

Warmth and gratitude flashed through her, bringing a lump to her throat. She swallowed hard, dislodging it.

"Here's your cue stick."

"Thanks." As she took the cue from Brandon, her fingers brushed his with nary a spark of the sort Johnny sent through her just by breathing. As if sensing her body was momentarily under control, Johnny took her arm again, steering her to the other side of the room and sending her pulse skittering through her veins.

"What would you like to drink—soda, fruit juice, lite beer . . .?"

"I'm good, thanks."

"What're we playing? 9-Ball?" asked Darrell.

"Straight pool, no calling. Let's make it easy on J," said Brandon.

Johnny snorted. "Ignore the jealousy swirling through the room and let a pro show you how it's done."

Everyone laughed except Tina, who was still stunned at where she was, who she was with, what she was doing. She, who loved the solitude of her nighttime job, devoid of people, was amongst some of the hottest specimens of mankind and interacting with them.

Her mouth dried as she watched Johnny, the hottest of the bunch, saunter up to the table and take position. One foot slightly in front of the other, knees bent, he leaned over the pool table with the cue resting in his hand. His hands mesmerized her as the shaft glided back and forth between his curled fingers, pushed and pulled by the hand gripping the butt, the action seeming to caress the polished wood instead of merely holding it.

So engrossed was she in the erotic movement of his hands, the quick stroke of the cue forward, that it barely registered that had he given it a bit more top-spin or used a long bridge and a complete follow-through, he would have pocketed more balls.

"Whoa, he got a ball in!" said Brandon.

"Two," corrected Darrell.

"A fluke," added Nino.

"That was skill, my man." Johnny turned to her.

"Your turn."

Tina turned her attention from Johnny to the table, noticing he'd pocketed the two and the six and had lined up the seven—a straight shot. And a boring shot that anyone could make. The ten, on the other hand, required that she put reverse English on the cue ball, making it kiss both the thirteen and the ten, before sending the ten rolling into the pocket.

Much more challenging. But more importantly, much more impressive. And she wanted to impress. Because what she lacked in looks, she made up for in skill, which would make her feel equal.

She stepped forward—and into her comfort zone.

Johnny stepped forward and took her arm. "See the seven?" He turned her away from her intended shot. "All you have to do is stand like this—"

Groans filled the room, followed by, "Don't listen to him" and "You'll do better on your own" and "Or blindfolded."

"Ignore them," Johnny said. "We are going to ace this."

"See? He thinks he's playing golf!" said Luke.

Tina smiled. The last bit of tension left her—until Johnny resumed his lessons.

"Are you right-handed?"

"Yes."

"Then place your left leg forward and bent slightly at the knee . . ."

His jeans accented the strength of his thigh in the most delicious way.

". . . as you lean across the table like this." He leaned across the table as he'd instructed.

She tried to keep from checking out his ass.

"—and hold the stick like this . . ." She stared at

his long fingers, wrapped around the cue, trying not to imagine them wrapped around her. "Push with your right hand. All the power, the control comes from the butt."

Unbidden, her gaze slipped to his, delectably displayed in his designer jeans. Yes, indeed, it most certainly did.

He straightened, motioning for her to try.

Tina took up the position, lined up the ball, and—

Johnny stepped behind her. His groin brushed her ass. His chest glanced her back. His fingers surrounded hers, as he positioned them.

"The side of the table is called the rail. You don't want to hit that for this shot. You want to keep the ball in the bed of the table."

The rich timbre of his instructions sounded like foreplay to her ears. Her body, vibrating from the nearness of him, craving to lean back and feel his groin against her, most definitely wanted to 'hit that' in a 'bed' that had nothing to do with pool and everything to do with sex.

"You want to stroke like this . . . " His hands guided hers, back and forth. The polished wood of the cue, sliding through the circle of her fingers, made her imagine another wood, sliding in and out in a different place.

". . . and lightly kiss the ball . . ."

The word 'kiss' rolled off his tongue and onto her body, taking her mind back to the kiss in his office that had barely gotten started.

His hand pulled back on the cue a little farther and then pushed slightly harder and his hips— unnecessarily—brushed her ass on the stroke toward the ball, causing Tina to jerk, which brought the tip of her cue down to hit the table.

A scratch.

Warmth rushed to her face. She'd scratched on the easiest shot ever invented.

Groans of sympathy filled the air.

"Nice try." Johnny released her hands and moved away. "We'll do better next time."

The words, like all the others before it, were spoken with the matter-of-factness of a teacher instructing a pupil, but the faint glimmer of amusement mixed with a sheen of smoky hotness in his eyes told the real story: He'd known exactly what he was doing and the effect it would have on her.

Why, that little—make that, *big*—fiend.

With a wink, he turned his attention to his friends. "Who's next?"

As the hormone surge flooding her body receded and the trembling from pent-up arousal subsided, Tina watched Johnny. He seemed relaxed—his smile natural, his gaze more open and less concealing, his body loose. Ironically, she'd stood in his office, wondering about the real Johnny in a romantic way, whereas now she was getting to see a glimpse of the real him in a deeper way. Because with his men, who seemed to genuinely like and respect him, he didn't seem to pretend, didn't seem to don the blank stare like a mask. With them he seemed to just *be*.

As if feeling her eyes on him, he turned. Laughter at something she hadn't been paying attention to shone in his eyes, lingering as he looked at her, slowly morphing into laughter directed at her. "Want to try again?"

Tina smiled, amazed to find that her smile, too, felt natural. That, other than the arousal singing through her body, she, too, felt relaxed. And happier in the company of people outside her loved ones than she could ever remember being.

"Oh, after your excellent instruction . . ." She walked to him and took the pool cue from his hands. "I'm ready to do this on my own."

Cheers filled the room.

She winked at Johnny and turned to the table.

~ ~ ~ ~

Johnny laughed, the force of it taking him somewhat by surprise, as he didn't do it much. Chuckled, yes. From-the-gut laughs, rarely.

And he could honestly say he was having fun. Pool with the guys was always a good time, a time to unwind, exchange x-rated puns, and talk shit. A short reprieve from thinking about anything important.

But he couldn't remember the last time it had felt fun.

He turned his attention back to Tina, in time to hear her say, "Bottom right corner pocket."

What the heck was she doing? There was no way to knock the ball into the corner pocket without making a bank shot and bouncing the cue ball off two rails. She bent over the table, lined up the cue ball and let Johnny know she planned to do exactly that.

She struck, executed the perfect two-rail bank shot, and pocketed the ball in the corner pocket.

Johnny caught his mouth before it dropped open.

The guys cheered.

"Bottom left corner pocket," Tina said.

Perhaps that last shot has been luck, but there was no way she could make this one. It would require a jump shot, where the cue ball would rise off the table and skip over the ten then hit the six, which would then need to hit the thirteen in a combination shot to knock the thirteen into the pocket.

The thirteen went in the pocket.

The cheers were deafening.

Johnny joined in, realizing he'd been had. "So you can't play, huh?"

Tina grinned. "I never said that. You assumed I couldn't, so I let you think it."

"Once again, J is living proof of what happens when one ASSumes."

Everyone laughed.

Johnny raised his cue.

Brandon pretended to duck.

"So, Tina, can you put the ten in the side pocket?" asked Nino.

Tina turned back to the table. "Yes."

"Wait, wait," said Darrell. "Let's take bets. Ten to one says she can't do it."

Johnny reached in his pocket and removed $10. "I'm saying she can."

He smiled at Tina.

She smiled back. Then she made the shot.

"Yes!" said Nino, high-fiving Brandon.

The dollars piled up, the challenges continued, and Tina beat every one. The irony wasn't lost on Johnny that guys who made their living getting bills tucked into their custom-made skivvies were tossing those same dollars onto the table to bet on an incognito pool shark.

A pool shark who seemed to be loving every minute of it.

Gone was the defensive stance that seemed to say, *I don't care what you think*, when he suspected she cared a lot about what people thought.

Maybe that was the attraction she held for him—that despite the intricate pattern of artistic swirls that decorated a part of her face, giving the illusion of a mask, she was transparent. What she felt, thought or wanted was mirrored on her face, though he'd be willing to give all the money he'd bet on her pool skills that she didn't know it.

Now, she was even more transparent. Her stance was relaxed, her face forgotten—evidenced by the fact that she tucked her hair behind her left ear—as she concentrated on her game, calculating angles and plotting strategies.

Confidence radiated from her. Her eyes sparkled. Her grin, when she made the shot or high-fived one of the guys or received a pat on the back, dazzled.

All of which made Johnny want her more than if she were standing in the room naked.

Which made no sense. She was an anomaly.

In his world, things were calculated.

His business was designed around dishing out fantasies that made women happy to make a profit, then creating bigger and better fantasies to bag even more profit.

His personal interactions with women were calculated. He scoped out those who would want nothing more than sex, gave it to them, and went back to business. An endless loop.

Nothing about Tina was calculated.

Cheers and groans interrupted his thoughts.

Tina chanted, "You know I'm bad, I'm bad—you know it," from Michael Jackson's, *Bad*, then gyrated her hips, doing a bad—in the literal sense—imitation of the King of Pop's pelvic thrusts.

All of which made him laugh and his cock twitch.

How the fuck could he laugh and feel the beginnings of a hard-on at the same time? Until that moment, he'd have thought the two mutually exclusive, since laughing was the last thing he felt when aroused.

She sent him her grin—a grin filled with pure enjoyment laced with arousal that hadn't completely gone away since that kiss.

The kiss. Another first.

How could a woman put so much passion into a simple nibble, the lightest touch of lips, making his cock harder than some of the most experienced lip locks?

His cock twitched again.

If he kept this up, he'd work up a full-fledged boner, which would not be cool in front of the guys. The ribbing would be merciless. Though it was probably already too late, since he'd had one when he thought he was teaching her to play. He didn't think she'd noticed, but Brandon's look had been knowing.

Which brought him back to the hard-on problem. Whether he actually had one at that moment was irrelevant. It was just a temporary reprieve. He'd been fighting—and losing—the battle against wanting her.

Because she was not his type.

Because she was *nice*.

Because she was those other words that he avoided at all costs—'wholesome' with a trace of 'innocence.'

All of which meant she was not a sex-only type.

None of which mattered. Because he still wanted her, still had to have her, if only one time. And the only way to justify that was to give her the fantasy date she'd asked for, making it the best one ever, thereby leaving her happy and fulfilled when it was over.

If you were nice, you'd just walk away.

But he was not nice.

Another round of cheering, with louder groans filled the air.

"All right, let's wrap it up," Johnny said. "We've got practice in the morning."

And I've got a seduction to get underway.

8

Tina watched the guys file out of the room, accepting their compliments and congratulations with a grin that felt so wide she feared she looked like the Cheshire Cat. The thrill of winning, the pride of accomplishment, the flush of acceptance bubbled through her bloodstream. Once they were gone, she practically twirled to face Johnny. "I won!"

Johnny, who was collecting beer bottles and putting away pool cues, laughed. "'Won' is an understatement." He raised his eyes to hers—eyes seemingly simmering with laughter and admiration and something sexy; eyes that were alive, the exact opposite of those belonging to the man in the photos.

She could lose herself in those eyes. She *wanted* to lose herself in them.

"How did you learn to play like that?"

His question pricked her happiness bubble. Going down that path would be a mood crusher, a sure-fire spoiler to the dream-like quality of the moment. Like Cinderella, she wanted this moment with her hunky

Prince to last until it had to end.

And she wanted the Prince. Before the proverbial midnight, before she lost the opportunity. Just once, so she would have a memory to cherish forever. Just once, she wanted to feel what other women—no, what her friend Sarah—rhapsodized about when she spent the night with a guy who hit all the right spots. What Tina had dreamt it would feel like with David.

Forget the candlelight, romantic music, whatever. Forget the fantasy *date*. It was time to be totally honest. She wanted fantasy *sex*.

There's no guarantee you'd get that with him.

No, there wasn't. But she felt she would. And even if she didn't, it couldn't be worse than David.

So she gave him the short answer. "From my father." Then she steered the conversation back to where she wanted it. On him. "Why do they tease you about your game? You're not that bad."

His lips quirked. "Thanks."

She laughed. "I didn't mean it quite like that. But, well, you can't be good at everything."

"There are a lot of things I'm not good at."

She watched his hand as it circled the bottle, seeing it on her flesh instead, cupping her leg as he lifted it, circling her arm as he pulled her to him. "Oh? Like what?" Her voice sounded light and flirty and teasing, just as she'd hoped.

"Cooking. Though I do make a killer cup of coffee." He sounded flirty right back.

She liked this Johnny and wanted to see more of him. "Okay. What else?"

"Horseback riding." He reached for an empty can, then paused and looked up. A half-smile lingered on his lips but his gaze was turned inward.

Tina watched, mesmerized, at the sight of yet another side of him.

"When I was eleven, I went with a group of boys from the Ho—" He stopped, as if he'd been about to say something he didn't mean to.

Tina wanted to know what he'd started to say, but held her tongue instead, waiting for him to continue.

". . . a group of boys from town. We were scared, one jockstrap away from peeing our pants, but punching each other on the shoulder, acting like it was no big deal."

Tina was enthralled. This was the longest time he'd talked and the most personal thing he'd shared.

"I had the misfortune of being first. I had barely gotten on my horse when Garrett, this kid who had always hated my guts, threw down a handful of bang snaps. The rapid pop-pop-pop, like a cap gun, spooked the horse and he took off. I was hanging on with everything I had while bouncing in that saddle like a human pogo stick."

He chuckled.

Tina joined in.

"My butt ached for a week."

"I bet."

He tossed the can in a bag and cocked his head toward her. The laughter faded from his eyes. "I'm also not good at this."

"This?" Her mind zipped back to the conversation they'd had in the office, when 'this' had meant the bet, the fantasy, and his participation in it all. She didn't think he was referring to that now.

"Innocent conversation."

Oh. That 'this.'

Whatever innocence had been present in the

conversation was completely gone, for there was nothing innocent in his voice. That one word hummed with its antonym, bringing the sexual tension that had hung in the air during the game whooshing back, thrumming her skin, turning the innocent thrill that had flooded her over winning into a wicked thrill of a different kind—the thrill of feeling him, skin against skin, heart against heart.

But it was his gaze that totally destroyed any illusion of innocence. The teasing glint as he'd acknowledged her winning was gone, as if it had never been there, replaced by an intensity that burned.

Tina took a deep breath.

This was her cue to make her move. To go after what she wanted. Him. Provided she could summon the courage to do so.

She drank in his gaze, letting it wash over her and through her, raising the speed of her heart, the rush of her pulse, mingling with the high of her pool victory still coursing through her veins, using it to make her daring enough to go after what she wanted.

"Well, then." She turned away and headed toward the door. She placed her hand on the pool table and trailed her fingertips along the rail, more out of a desperate need to keep her balance, to stop the shakiness in her legs from toppling her, than any attempt to be sexy or coy.

At the door, she reached for the light switch, pausing for a moment as she noticed her trembling fingertips, then flicked off the light and turned back to Johnny.

Like the room, Johnny was in shadow, which meant she was in shadow, too, illuminated only by the city lights sparkling through the windows along the east wall. She drew strength from the darkness—darkness in which she could be beautiful and whole and as perfect as the man in front of her. "Perhaps we can find something to do that you *are* good at."

Though it came out only slightly louder than a whisper, her voice seemed to bounce off the glass and echo in the silent, seductive gloom.

As Tina walked toward him, the shakiness in her hands spread to her chest, causing jerky breaths to spill from her lips.

She couldn't believe she was there, in that room, in front of that man—a man who less than a week ago had literally been a figment of her imagination. Even in her most fevered imaginings, she'd never dreamt she would be doing what she was about to do now.

She was making the kill shot. Going after the game ball.

And the thrill of the game had never, ever felt so exhilarating.

With each step, anticipation fueled the trembling in her body, excitement caused her ragged breaths, nervousness added a delicious edge to her desire until all too soon she was in front of Johnny.

Johnny stood still, unmoving, as if frozen. But he was far from frozen. As her gaze traveled up, past the alluring curve of his neck, his muscles contracted, moving his Adam's apple forward as he swallowed. As she admired the curve of his jaw, it clenched and unclenched. As she let her gaze drift to his nose, his nostrils flared with each breath—breaths which sounded softly jagged, forming a chorus of need and desire with hers.

Or so she hoped.

Just as she hoped that the stillness, the tension in

his body that she felt as his heat enveloped her, meant they shared the same erotic thoughts and images, and the rapid workings of his throat and his chest meant he was as aroused as she was.

Which she would know, once and for all, when she looked into his eyes.

Despite the decadent sensations roiling through her body, her courage faltered, preventing her gaze from traveling higher than his nose.

What if the desire was there but it was mingled with pity? What if he was aroused and willing but his gaze said this was charity sex?

She laughed inwardly. Yeah, right. Like he was so hard up for women he needed to take advantage of charity sex.

She knew she was being silly but she couldn't help it, couldn't help David's parting gift of insecurity from surfacing. But she couldn't risk meeting Johnny's gaze—because maybe, instead of pity, she'd see something else that she didn't want to see.

So she didn't look. She looked at his mouth instead. His soft, succulent lips. "Are you good at this?" It was the barest sound, whispered so close to his lips that she felt her breath return to her, hot with need.

She tilted her head, leaned closer, and placed her lips against his. They were as soft as before—but unmoving.

I don't know what I'm doing. What if he doesn't like it? What if he's not moving because he's getting ready to push me away? Maybe I should have looked into his eyes and—

She shut off her mind and nibbled his lower lip, suckling, loving the way it felt in her mouth. Gaining courage from his sharp intake of breath, she slanted her head and leaned closer, pressing her body against his, feeling her breasts flatten against his chest and her nipples brush against his hard pecs, sending heat spiraling to her stomach and spreading to her core. She moved her lips against his like he had done to hers in the office and jutted her hips forward.

And felt proof that she had been right.

A thrill of erotic victory zoomed through her. She removed her lips from his, letting the confidence infused by his arousal leak into her voice. "Or are you good at—"

Her words were arrested by the growl that seemed to rumble through him, then stolen by his mouth as he raised his hand to the back of her head and pulled her forward, pressing his lips against hers, taking control of the kiss.

Though what she'd called a kiss before Johnny was laughable. Unlike David's wet kiss and the few unmemorable experiences after him, this was a *kiss*. Johnny's lips took hers, devouring, possessing. She gasped into his mouth, in awe that it could be like this, that the simple movement of lips touching could spark such heat in parts of her body far away from her head, heat that speared her stomach like the most delicious of punches, spreading the most tantalizing pain, before snaking downward and throbbing between her thighs.

On the tail end of her gasp, while she was marveling at the simple action of his lips, his tongue entered her mouth, sending another wave of wonder, along with a shockwave of desire, through her. Her tongue met his, tentatively exploring and tasting, then deeply probing, emboldened by his urgency, excited by the ragged breaths that matched the desperate search of his tongue.

Tina slipped her hands under his t-shirt, anxious to feel the flesh that he'd teased her with. She ran her fingertips up his back, marveling at the smoothness, the muscled strength—and becoming impatient.

It wasn't enough.

She grabbed the bottom of the cotton and pulled upward, breaking the kiss when cloth touched her chin.

His hands replaced hers, seemingly equally impatient, and yanked the shirt up and off.

She felt a pang of disappointment that she couldn't see clearly, that she'd turned the lights out and missed the opportunity to appreciate his beauty to the fullest. But him not being able to see her fully, so she could lose herself in the feeling and not have it interrupted by self-consciousness over her face, had been more important.

He tossed the shirt onto the floor, then pulled her closer by sliding his palm along her cheek.

Her left cheek.

Tina stiffened and instinctively jerked her face away. "No."

Johnny paused.

Oh, no. Why did she have to do that, the very thing she had taken steps to prevent? But she hadn't counted on him touching her, hadn't practiced her reaction and, because of that, had probably just ruined everything. She looked away. "I'm sorry. I—"

Johnny placed a finger against her lips, the touch seemingly aimed at shushing, not arousing, then turned her around so her back was to him.

Tina breathed a sigh of relief. She hadn't ruined things. He understood.

His hands pulled the hair back from her face—the good side—seconds before his lips caressed her jaw. Tina inhaled sharply, tilting her head left, giving him full access. As his mouth moved downward, nibbling along the curve of her neck, her exhale ended in a moan.

While his mouth trailed kisses across her shoulder, his hand moved to her back. She heard the scratch of her zipper, felt her bra loosen and his fingers slide both sets of straps from her shoulders.

Suddenly, she was free.

She looked down at the dim outline of her breasts, noticing her turgid nipples pointing toward the door. An illicit thrill shot through her. How decadent to be topless in an office, where anyone could come in, where—

Johnny's hands slipped under her breasts, cupping them, stealing all thought away from what someone could see to what he was doing.

She arched her back, jutting her breasts into his hands and her ass against his groin, needing more of the feel of him and his hardness.

Johnny gasped against her neck.

A moan slipped from her throat. David had treated her breasts like rising bread dough, kneading and squeezing. Johnny treated them like the erogenous zones they were, caressing her sensitive areola with the pads of his forefingers and squeezing them, massaging them, and rubbing her nipples against his palms, sending spears of heat outward and downward. This was what she'd wanted to feel, when she'd lain alone in her bed at night, imagining someone holding her, fondling her. She'd imagined the touch driving her mad with need.

Just like this.

Only, it wasn't nearly enough. She had waited so long for more than this.

His hands slid to her waist.

Her hands slid to her pocket, fumbling, searching . . . finding. She held the condom between her fingertips and held it toward him. "Here." Her voice was a hoarse croak.

He took it, took a step back, breaking the contact with their bodies. Foil crinkled, a zipper rasped, clothing rustled, and then he was back, his mouth back on her neck, his hands back on her breasts, fondling their fullness, pinching her ripeness, forcing a groan from her throat and a gyration of her hips.

His hands slid up her thighs. His fingers stoked her desire and her dress caressed her starved flesh on the way up.

As his fingers slid into the sides of her panties, his chest pressed against her back, pressing her forward, bending her over the table.

Her panties slid down to the floor.

Her dress slid up over her hips.

Johnny's lips touched hers. She turned her head farther to the side so she could kiss him more fully. While his mouth continued to plunder hers, her heart continued to pound and every nerve in her body seemed to be alive, sending wave after wave of sensation to every part of her body—lips, mouth, breasts, nipples, stomach, hips, pussy—especially her pussy.

Until his fingers found her wetness and stroked and rubbed the hard nub. Every sensation roiling through her body instantly coalesced at her pussy, overwhelming her.

It was too much. She was seconds away from climaxing and they'd just started. She'd wanted to draw it out, to linger and enjoy and make it last. But the wait had been so long, the need had built so strong. There was no denying it.

"Oh, yes." Her pussy throbbed and pulsed.

"Oh, yes." Her muscles tightened, making one last effort to hold back.

"Oh, fuck," said Johnny.

His cock nudged her wetness.

As she came, every sensation broke free, sending rolling waves of quakes and trembles flooding her body, merging a string of words into a single strangled epiphany. "Thisismyfantasy."

"Not fantasy." Johnny's voice was strained. "Reality."

The tip of his cock entered her. "Oh, fuck." He breathed the word against her back, more of a plea than a curse. He pressed forward. His cock entered another inch. "Fuck." This time, the word was filled with pain.

He felt so big, filling her entrance while he was barely in. A flicker of fear merged with the subsiding quivers. Maybe he was too big. Or maybe she was too small. Maybe after all this, maybe he—they— wouldn't fit. Maybe—

He withdrew, then pushed forward, thrusting the word 'maybe' from her mind.

He withdrew, then pushed forward, forcing *every* word and thought from her mind, narrowing her world to just him, to just his cock, and to how indescribably fantastic he felt.

And then he was in, his chest resting against her back, his breath fast and ragged as if he had just run a marathon. "Don't. Move."

Her mind barely registered the words, still stunned to find him inside her, reveling in the feel of him and the way he completely filled her, awed by the feel of her walls completely surrounding him. She clenched her muscles, seeking to draw him even closer.

"Ahh, fuck." This 'fuck' was a groan of apology as his inertia was broken. He raised himself off her back and gripped her hips with both hands. He withdrew—this time all the way out—and entered, this time all the way in. First slow, then faster, then even faster.

The sensation she thought was gone came back in a rush.

With each thrust, the feel of him inside of her, the jiggle of her breasts, the erotic image of her spread atop a pool table with him gripping her ass and pummeling her body, the power over causing his lack of control, the powerlessness of her inability to move, drove her arousal higher, pounding her body with desire, sending it climbing and spiraling and building inside her.

She whimpered and clawed at the table.

He grunted and gripped her hips tighter.

She screamed as the second orgasm rocked her body.

He groaned and then froze as his cock jerked inside her.

A few seconds later, he withdrew. His chest once again met her back, his arms looped around her waist, and he kissed her lightly across the shoulders. Their jagged breaths mingled and then calmed simultaneously, bringing with it the reality of what she had just done.

She had just had sex that was better than she'd ever imagined with a man she never would have imagined it possible to have sex with.

She'd had her fantasy. And, at that moment, while tremors rippled through her body and the weight of him against her kept the memory of him intensely alive, she believed that Johnny was right: Having, enjoying, *living* the fantasy *was* better than having nothing at all. She just hoped she felt the same way tomorrow and every day thereafter.

It was time to leave, time to return to reality. And she wanted to do so without ruining the last vestiges of the fantasy with awkward conversation or meaningless pleasantries or promises.

She stirred under him, signaling that she wanted to get up. He got the message and lifted himself off of her.

She dressed.

He dressed.

Thankfully, in silence.

When she was finished, she smiled, turned to Johnny and said, "Thank you," before turning toward the door.

It was only after she left that she realized she had never once looked him in the eyes.

9

"Thank you."

Johnny stared at the two simple words on the invoice from Club Boudoir for Hot Dreams' upcoming show. But he wasn't thinking about the printed words on a piece of paper. He was thinking of the spoken words, softly uttered in a husky voice, in the poolroom.

While Club Boudoir's words were standard politesse, Tina's had been seemingly sincere. While Club Boudoir's were expected business etiquette, Tina's were unexpected, and unexpectedly insulting. As if she, like Club Boudoir, was thanking him for his business—or, rather, his services.

As if he were, indeed, that whore he'd told her he wasn't.

Not that he thought she'd meant it that way. But you didn't thank someone for fucking you as you left. Well, perhaps in a flirty, lighthearted, let's-do-it-again sometime kind of way. But not in some kind of serious, sincere way.

That was in the Handbook of Fucking Etiquette.

If her tone had been flirty and light-hearted, would that have made a difference?

Probably not. He'd still be pissed.

He pushed himself from his desk in irritation and swiveled his chair toward the window, staring sightlessly out over downtown Seattle and Puget Sound, ignoring the view that he knew he was paying too much for.

Why was he pissed? More importantly, why the hell was he even thinking about her?

He didn't think about women. He fucked—*when* he fucked, which wasn't often recently, another inexplicable mystery—and it was over. Both of them were satisfied until the next time they hooked up—*if* they hooked up—or until they no longer wanted to hook up.

He wanted another hookup with Tina.

Only 'hookup' didn't seem like the right word. Maybe 'redo' was more accurate.

'Redo' is right. Your performance sucked. You almost came, right out of the gate, like an inexperienced teenager.

Johnny's face warmed with embarrassment at the memory. But, damn, she'd been so tight and so wet. After all the time spent working it in inch-by-inch, by the time he was in, he felt like they'd been at it slowly for hours. And then she did that clench thing like the Mistress of Kegel, and he'd almost lost it. He couldn't remember ever feeling that. Not even when he *was* a teenager.

His cock lengthened at the memory—and at the idea of feeling it again.

Then, after your stellar performance, you stood there stupidly, like a tongue-tied adolescent.

He'd been silent because he hadn't known what to say. Literally. His usual witty repartee would have sounded as insulting to her as her 'thank you' had been to him.

Yeah, well, that was only partly responsible for his silence. The main reason was because he'd felt like an ass—he'd taken her from behind, bent over a pool table, for fuck's sake.

Yeah, sure, as already noted, that's what he did. Fuck. The women he got with were after a good fuck and the 'where' and the 'how' didn't matter. But with Tina, something about the 'where' felt wrong, despite the fact that she'd come on to him, and the 'how' felt wrong, even though taking her from behind was his way of trying to make her forget about her face.

And back to your performance. As previously noted, you didn't even give her a good fuck.

Ahh, hell. He needed a redo, where he would do *everything* right this time. If only to shut up his ego and return his focus to business where it belonged.

He turned from the window and returned to his desk, going through the property management file until he came to another invoice with the words "Thank you" stamped on it. He dialed.

"Plants Alive," said the woman he couldn't get out of his mind.

"Hey. It's Johnny."

There was a long pause.

"Johnny?" Her voice was a breathy lilt of surprise.

She wasn't the only one surprised.

"I mean . . . Johnny, hi . . . Um, what can I do for you? I mean, is there a problem with your plants?"

A plant emergency. That made him chuckle.

"Oh, God. No, no, of course not." She sounded

embarrassed. She heaved a big sigh. "I'm sor—"

"What're you doing tonight?"

"Oh. Well. Watering your plants."

"They'll survive." He paused, injecting a note of casualness into his tone, as if he asked the question every day, when in fact, he never did. He then added a dose of no-big-deal, which was true. It wasn't a big deal.

That so? Then why don't you ask other women?

He shrugged off the question.

"Why don't we grab a bite to eat, instead?"

~ ~ ~ ~

Oh my God, Oh my God. He's asking me out. The man I had the mind-blowing sex with and never expected to hear from again just asked me out ON A DATE.

Tina suppressed the desire to let out a seventeen-year-old-girl squeal.

She'd replayed their night together over and over, reliving every titillating second, from the pool game to pool sex. She was thankful that, just as she'd hoped, she had experienced what other women had—and what many probably hadn't—and what she had always dreamt of. As she had hoped, she had memories to cherish. As she had hoped, she still believed that Johnny was right, that living the fantasy had been way better than never having experienced it.

But, no matter how many times she tried, she couldn't stop herself from hoping against hope for just one more time.

And here he was. Her wish had been granted.

She had no illusions that it meant anything, but she was excited to have another opportunity. She might as well make it a date to remember—the fantasy date she had asked for—doing something she'd never done with anyone. Summoning a tone of indifference she didn't feel, she said, "Brianna will be with my mom. Why don't you come over for dinner, instead?"

After a pause during which Tina feared he was going to say no, he said, "Sure."

"Say, seven-thirty?"

"Sure."

She gave him her address in a daze and hung up. Seven hours. She had to get someone to cover for her, go grocery shopping, cook, not to mention figure out what she was going to wear, and—

What had she been thinking?

She grabbed her cell phone and made a call. "Hi, Mom."

"Hi, honey."

"Can you keep Brianna tonight?"

"I always keep Brianna on Friday nights."

"I meant overnight, at your place. I'm, uh, taking your advice and Brianna's and being social."

"Oh, honey. That's wonderful. Are you going out with Sarah?"

"No, Sarah's still in Italy. It's a . . . new friend." While it wasn't exactly a lie, she felt bad saying it to her mother.

"Oh? Who? Where did you—"

She was not going to go there. "Mom, I'm kind of in a hurry. I'll tell you about everything tomorrow, okay?"

"Okay. I have Zumba class in the morning so I'll bring her back by eleven."

"Sounds good."

"I am so happy you are going out. Have fun, baby."

Oh, I so will. "Thanks, Mom. Love you. Bye."

The afternoon passed in a blur. With so much to do, there was no time to think or react to what was about to happen. But now, with only twenty minutes to spare, butterflies had made an appearance.

Tina leaned over the bathroom sink, staring into the mirror as she added another coat of mascara. She usually didn't wear makeup but, just as she'd worn the rare dress for the visit to Johnny's office, she was donning makeup for him, too. Not much. Just mascara and a bit of tinted lip gloss. For her, that was a lot.

She smoothed her dress down over her hips. The last one had been subtly flattering, but this one was a blood red, in-your-face, sex-me-up dress. It molded itself to her curves, with a bodice that dipped low to reveal a healthy amount of cleavage and a hemline cut high to show off a significant amount of thigh. Sarah had bought it for her on her birthday, telling Tina every woman should always have a just-in-case dress in her closet. Tina had protested that she would never need it.

And here she was, wearing it.

Though, truth be told, she didn't think she would've had the guts to wear it if she hadn't already slept with Johnny.

Slept with.

Tina laughed. Now, there was a misnomer. What they'd done was about as far from sleeping as one could get. And on a pool table, no less.

Tina's face warmed. She still couldn't believe she'd done that. To go from no sex to propositioning a guy with sex on a pool table . . . Her boldness surprised her and, truth be told, filled her with pride. She'd gone after what she wanted and gotten it.

And, oh Lord, had she gotten it.

Her fevered pre-Johnny fantasies had been so tame, namely missionary position amid tangled sheets. Who knew sex from behind could be so . . . raw and passionate and exciting and—

The doorbell rang.

The butterflies took flight, fluttering around her stomach until she opened the door. At the sight of Johnny, they dropped to the pit of her stomach, taking her breath with them.

He looked stunning in an expensive-looking black leather jacket in the softest hide, tailored black slacks, and a red shirt, which complemented his black hair and the warm cinnamon undertones in his skin. "Wow," she said.

"Wow," he repeated. His tone was teasing but his eyes smoldered as they traveled over her body, lingering at the skin-revealing places, as if imagining her as an item on the menu, instead of the food she'd prepared.

She remembered her manners. "Come in," she said. She stepped aside and he entered, the heat of his body once again caressing her with his nearness, snapping her mind back to what it had felt like to touch and feel his skin under her fingers. The smell of him—the same woodsy and spicy and exotic scent with subtle notes of simply him—enveloped her, fueling the urge to lean closer, feeding the desire to bury her face in the curve of his neck for a closer whiff, a light taste.

You're being ridiculous. Don't make a fool of yourself!

One way or another, she was destined to make a fool of herself. How was she going to get through a simple date, a simple dinner, and act normal?

For starters, close the door and move away.

She did, then realized she didn't know how to greet him. Was she supposed to kiss him? Hug him? Shake hands? Do nothing?

He decided for her, leaning in for a one-arm hug and a kiss on her cheek—her good cheek. It was all she could do not to lean forward, press against him, and turn her head to capture his lips and resume where they left off last week.

"Something smells good." The words bounced along her cheek.

"Oh, it's herbed lamb shanks in a wine sauce."

"I wasn't referring to food."

"Oh." Her pulse skittered.

"But the lamb smells good, too."

"Thank you."

He handed her a bag. "For the hostess."

She took it from him, grateful for the distraction it provided, and removed the tissue-wrapped package. She unwrapped it—and laughed. "A picture frame?"

"I didn't know if you liked wine. This I know you like."

Her fingertip traced the embossed cacti dotting the border, touched that he hadn't brought one of the typical things one brings to dinner, but instead, something unique to her. Such a small gesture and yet . . . A lump formed in her throat. It was the first time a man had given her a gift.

It doesn't mean anything.

She knew that. But the lump remained.

You're being ridiculous. Don't make a fool of yourself!

She swallowed hard and smiled, though she couldn't meet his gaze, her full attention on putting the tissue back in the bag. "I will be taking photos of

Brianna at a school performance coming up. This will be perfect for it. Thank you."

She distracted herself with a change in topic. "Come on back." She turned and headed toward the living room.

The distance should have dimmed the awareness, but instead worsened it. Because now, as she led him down the hall, she wondered if his eyes were on her, roving her body, watching the sway of her hips, perhaps remembering how he had gripped them, pulling them forward and back, how her ass had slapped against his groin with the force of his movement, how he had groaned, how—

She forced the thoughts away and concentrated on walking, putting one foot in front of the other, determined that this—falling flat on her face—would not be how she made a fool of herself. She was being a big enough fool as it was with her thoughts. *She* was the only one remembering that night. *She* was the one with the vivid imagination, thinking that he would be looking at her ass and fantasizing about what they'd done. *He* was probably checking out the photos of her and Brianna along the wall or mentally questioning—or maybe even liking—her bold paint color choices accenting the walls.

Or, most likely, not even thinking about anything related to her at all.

Arriving in the living room, she said, "Dinner's almost ready. Please have a seat while I get drinks," then turned to him. "What would you like . . ."

The air whooshed out of her. Unless he'd been admiring her hardwood flooring, his eyes *had* been on her ass, for they slowly moved upwards, caressing her waist, lingering on her breasts before meeting her gaze.

His eyes were dark and hot.

"Something red." His voice was sexy.

"Wine?" Her voice was breathless.

He dipped his head. "For starters."

Oh, Lord. That had not helped her blood. Heart racing, she practically fled to the kitchen. She set the frame on the counter, turned off the stove, popped the baked potatoes into the microwave, and poured two glasses of wine. By the time she made it back to Johnny, her calm was restored.

Somewhat.

He was standing by the fireplace, looking at the photos on the wall.

She handed him the glass, once again keeping her fingers from touching his and reigniting the heat sparking through her body that she'd barely gotten under control.

"Your daughter?"

"Yes."

"She looks like you."

Tina took a sip of wine and looked at the wall, at photos she knew by heart, every detail etched in her memory. Brianna's first birthday party. Five years old and sitting on grandma's lap. Her first grade school picture, grinning wide with a gaping smile, showing off her first lost tooth. Her first solo ballet performance when she was eight . . .

Tina smiled. "A little. But she's . . . " *flawless* " . . . beautiful." Inside and out, a perfect little being who continued to delight and surprise her, even on the days when she was far from angelic. Pride swelled in Tina's heart.

"And that's Brianna with my mom."

Johnny turned back to the photos, a small smile on his face as he glanced at the one she pointed to. "Nice." His gaze traveled to the rest. He turned his head back to her, brow raised in a sexy way.

"But none of Brianna with her dad?"

Tina stiffened.

Johnny waited.

"No."

"And none with you?"

For Brianna's sake, there were photos with Tina. They just weren't displayed. She forced a smile. "I don't like photos of me."

He reached forward and traced her lip with his fingertip, relaxing lips that she didn't know she'd tightened, releasing a gasp she didn't know she was holding in, sending heat she thought she'd doused sizzling through her body.

"And you don't like these questions."

It was more of a statement than a question, but she answered it anyway. "No."

"Then what should we talk about?"

"You."

His fingers continued to stroke.

Her body continued to spark.

"What about me?"

Why did you want to see me again? "Why don't you dance any more?"

He laughed, a low husky sound that caressed her eardrums. His fingertip moved to the corner of her mouth, and joined by the others, on to her jaw, then back to her neck. His palm cupped her cheek, drawing her head upward, seconds before he bent toward her. His lips stopped mere inches from hers. "Is that really what you want to know?"

He kissed the corner of her mouth.

Tina gasped.

"Right here?" His lips moved, nibbling along her jaw, nipping her earlobe.

Tina shivered.

"Right now?"

Her body quaked with tremors, sparked by his breath bouncing off her skin. His words stroked her mind, making the answer to her question—or any question—the last thing she wanted. 'Right here' and 'right now,' her desire for verbal communication had evaporated, replaced by physical desire.

Yes, she wanted an answer to her question—questions—but . . .

She tilted her head to the left, giving her neck to him.

He took her gift, following the curve with his mouth, kissing and licking lightly.

Tina moaned softly in the back of her throat, instinctively leaning forward and pressing against him, feeling his chest against hers as she'd craved to do ever since he'd walked through the door.

His lips left her neck and returned to her mouth, moving over hers, demanding a response that she was only too happy to give, igniting desire that had been simmering within her all week.

The microwave dinged, alerting her that the potatoes were done, jerking her out of wanton hussy mode and back to the role of polite hostess.

She pulled back with a shaky laugh. "Dinner. I completely forgot. Would you like to eat?"

"Yes."

She shrugged away a pang of disappointment, stepped back, and turned to lead the way to the kitchen.

He grabbed her hand, stopping her. "Not lamb." His eyes, hooded and dark, roved her, letting her know exactly what he would like to eat.

A thrill shot through her. Pleasure nipped her heart. Dinner could wait.

Still holding his hand, she turned in the opposite direction and led the way to her bedroom, no longer worried about tripping. This time, she imagined his thoughts having everything to do with her—her hips, her ass—and all the things he wanted to do to her. Or better yet, all the things she wanted to do to him.

She entered her room, let go of him, and went to the windows, drawing the curtains for privacy— against those looking in and against Johnny looking closely at her. She left the lamp on the nightstand turned on, only so she could see her way back to him and see him in its dim glow.

He was standing there watching her, still looking hungry.

She stopped in front of him. "I want you to stand there, just like that." She unbuttoned his shirt, enjoying the silky material brushing her knuckles, the anticipation brushing her nerve endings. Last time had been rushed. This time she wanted to savor every touch, every sensation.

The last button popped free. She slipped her fingers under the soft cotton and pushed it off his shoulders and down around his arms, where the material caught around his wrists. She rubbed her hands over his chest, enjoying the feel of the hard nubs of his nipples stabbing her palms, loving the rounded ridges of muscle lining his stomach, marveling at the fact that there was not a single ounce of flab. She slid her palms down his arms, fingertips circling his muscular biceps, triceps, or whatever-ceps, uncaring about what they were called, only caring about how they felt.

Soft and smooth skin.

She squeezed.

Sinewy and strong muscle.

She dropped her hands to his wrists and the material bunched around them, the still-buttoned cuffs preventing the shirt from dropping to the floor.

Bound and immobile man.

A thrill shot through her. He was hers for the teasing, the exploring, the touching, the *taking*.

She smoothed the pads of her fingers along his waist, dipping under the lip of the waistband of his pants, lightly raking the tips of her fingernails against his flesh. His muscles quivered.

Because of her actions? She did it again.

His muscles quivered again.

The noticeable tent in the front of his slacks jerked.

She acted. He reacted. She loved it—the thrill of it, the power of it—and wanted more. To do more, to see more, to feel more.

She unbuckled his belt and unzipped his pants, loving the feel of his hardness against her knuckles and the rasp of his breath against her forehead, the jerky movement of his chest.

His pants, aided by the weight of his belt, the slight nudge of her fingers, and the welcome effects of gravity, dropped to the floor, revealing his firm hips, granite thighs, and very pronounced bulge.

Her breath caught in her chest, mingled with the erratic beat of her heart, and sent waves of need outward, moving her to act on her craving for more.

She hooked her fingers into the front of his black briefs and pulled them away from his delicious bulge, uncovering the tip of what she most wanted to see, before sliding back to the side and pulling them over his hips and down his thighs, where they joined the pants pooling around his ankles.

And there he stood, gloriously naked and titillatingly hard, and more exciting than anything she'd ever seen in photos or video. He twitched, seemingly calling for her attention, beckoning her to touch.

She smoothed her hand down the flat plane of his groin, stopping when she reached the juncture of his cock, before wrapping her fingers around the base of it, moving outward, and encircling all of him.

He grunted.

She gasped, awed by the feel, so soft and yet hard, so silky and yet warm, resting against the palm of her hand.

She stroked outward.

His cock jerked in her hand. He cursed.

A tiny pearl of liquid glistened at the head, tempting her to move her head closer and lower and . . . did she dare? . . . taste its tanginess or saltiness or muskiness.

All words she had read in books to describe it, but she had no idea if it was true.

She wanted to know for sure, not guess by reading.

She glanced up at him, seeking permission.

His body was tense. His jaw was clenched. He was looking down, his hooded eyes intently focused on her fingers, as if willing them into action with the force of his stare. When that failed, as she remained motionless, his cock slid between her fingers, thrust forward by the groin that now butted the front of her hand.

Her attention returned to his cock, straining, reaching, yet captive in her palm.

His need gave her the permission she sought.

Tina slipped her dress from her shoulders and down over her hips before stepping out of it and kicking off her shoes, joining him in his nakedness.

His eyes darkened with hunger, feeding her hunger.

His cock seemed to grow harder in her hand, increasing her desire to taste him.

His breathing seemed harsher, causing her breath to shudder from her chest.

Bracing her free hand against his hip, Tina knelt in front of him, mouth-level with the glistening eye of his cock. She stuck out her tongue and flicked it against the tip, lapping up the tiny droplet.

He groaned.

She retracted her tongue, swirling it around her mouth, seeking the correct adjectives—tangy, with a hint of musk.

She wanted more of him, a bigger taste that would take all of him in her mouth. While she had never given head, she wasn't completely ignorant of the mechanics. After reading about it, she'd been curious to know what doing it actually looked like, so she'd watched a soft porn video at a porn-for-women site.

Seeing it had excited her. But not nearly as much as the mere thought of it with Johnny did.

She leaned forward again, this time slipping the tip of him inside, sucking lightly, swirling her tongue around the side, tracing the head, licking the curved ridge.

"You're killing me." The words trailed from his lips on the end of a groan.

She looked up at him, noting that he did look on the verge of dying—from need. Like the act of holding back, of remaining still was, indeed, killing him.

The ability to cause such intense need thrilled her.

Despite the submissive position, she felt equal—physically equal, for from that angle, her birthmark was invisible—and powerful, power-filled. She had the ability to give him intense pleasure and make him tremble with need.

She wanted to experience her power to the max. "Tell me what to do," she said, wrapping her lips around him, swirling her tongue along him, and taking him in until the tip of his head touched the back of her throat.

"That. Do that."

Emboldened, she reversed direction, sucking and licking, until his cock broke free with a soft, wet, pop.

"Oh, fuck."

Taking his pained curse as a sign of encouragement, she did it again. And again. Slowly in, slowly out, as deep as she could.

She stroked him with one hand, fondled his balls with the other, all the while sucking. She picked up the pace, moving faster.

"Stop." With a muttered curse, he took a step back and grabbed her head, pushing her gently away. She barely registered that his cock was no longer in her mouth before his shirt was off and she found herself scooped up into his arms and carried toward the bed.

"Wait."

He stopped.

"In the drawer. Condoms."

Still holding her, he leaned down and opened the drawer, then paused.

Straining to see what had caused his hesitation, Tina turned and looked down. Her face heated at the sight of the colorful boxes, imagining how that must look.

Extra Strength, Extra Sensitive, Ribbed, Studded, Large, XXL . . .

She'd wanted the night to be perfect. "I didn't know what kind you liked." *Or what I would like.*

He laughed—the from-the-gut kind that took her by surprise and that would've filled her with delight, if she hadn't felt so humiliated.

"Neon Glow."

"What? Oh, I don't have—"

"I'm joking." He reached down with one hand and grabbed a loose condom from the opened box—the box she'd bought for that night in the poolroom—then laid her on the bed.

As he ripped opened the condom, her eyes toured him hungrily, watching in anticipation.

He removed the condom and placed it at the tip of his cock. His attention was totally focused on his action. Her attention was totally focused on him. Who knew putting on a condom could be so sexy? Or perhaps it was knowing what he was going to do with it that made it so hot.

She reached over and flicked off the light, casting the room in darkness, which prevented her from seeing more than the silhouette of his shape. Not seeing disappointed her, but just like in the poolroom, hiding herself was more important.

The bed dipped.

Though she couldn't see him well, she could feel him. She reached up and placed the palms of her hands on his chest. The same chest that she'd felt in the light felt bigger in the dark. She looped her hands around his neck and her legs around his hips, pulling him down. She reveled in the feel of his body against hers, the feel of her nipples pressed against his, the feel of his cock nestled between her thighs.

It was exquisite. It was shocking. It was a jolt of sensation that took her breath away.

He leaned back and lowered his head to her neck. His lips followed its curve, nibbling and licking, sending tingles that made her gasp, before moving lower to her chest. He cupped a breast in his hand and drew her to his mouth, sucking and licking, then tweaking the nipple. Darts of pleasure trickled out over her breasts and down her stomach, straight to her pussy.

She arched toward him, wanting to be deeper in his mouth.

She wiggled her hips, wanting him to be inside her.

His mouth left her nipple and moved to her mouth, capturing it, plundering, possessing, demanding. His tongue traced the line of her lips. His cock crested her entrance.

And in a single instant, his cock entered her pussy and his tongue speared her mouth.

Tina gasped.

Her back arched.

Her hands clenched.

At the shock—the delicious, decadent shock—of him filling her.

She opened her eyes—eyes she didn't realized she'd closed—seeing little but the shadow of him. But she felt all of him—the tense muscles of his forearms pressed against her side, holding his weight off her; the feel of his hard cock buried deep inside of her.

His hips remained unmoving as his hand moved to her neck, his thumbs caressing the side of her jaw.

Her *left* jaw.

Tina tensed, despite the fact that it *felt* normal to the touch. Despite the fact that he could probably see little.

Her hand automatically flew to his, trying to pull it away.

"No," automatically escaped her lips.

He slid his hand from under hers, then cradled it in his and lifted it above her head. He repeated the action with the other hand, holding both captive in his one, before leaning across her body toward the nightstand.

Light burst into the room.

Tina froze.

Johnny's free hand returned to her neck. His finger traced her jaw, before moving upward and making S-like movements as if following curving lines. All the while, his eyes followed the strokes made by his fingers.

Tina couldn't move. She couldn't breathe. Tears filled her eyes. "Please. Don't."

His fingers continued stroking.

His eyes continued following.

Hurt stabbed Tina's heart. Why was he doing this? *How* could he do this? How could *he* be so mean and cruel, just as David had been?

Tears spilled from her eyes and rolled down her

cheeks.

The pad of Johnny's thumb smoothed the tears away from her blemished skin. "It's okay." His voice was soft. The palm of his hand gently cradled her flawed cheek.

No. Johnny wasn't being cruel, he was being caring.

He was nothing like David.

David had wanted darkness; Johnny wanted light.

David hadn't looked at her face, let alone touched it; Johnny was doing both.

Johnny dipped his head toward her, replacing his fingers with his lips and nibbling her imperfect skin with his perfect mouth.

David's lack of contact made her feel scorned; Johnny's touch made her feel cherished.

"You're a freak," Sam had yelled laughingly when she'd approached David the next day and David had turned away.

"You're beautiful," Johnny breathed in her ear.

His cock twitched inside her.

A soft sob escaped Tina's throat.

All her life, she'd wanted to feel normal and beautiful and desirable.

Now she did.

When she'd looked at the women in Johnny's photos, she'd wanted to be them.

Now she was.

Johnny reared back, holding himself off of her, and stared down at her. His eyes traveled her face before meeting her gaze.

When she'd looked at Johnny in his photos, she'd wondered if heat or passion or emotion ever shone in his eyes . . .

They all were there now. His look was caring as his gaze traveled her face.

She had wanted to see the real Johnny.

She was looking at him now.

As his hips began to move, the arousal that had been simmering in his eyes flared to life. As his cock stroked her core, his eyes dared her to look away.

Tina didn't look away—*couldn't* look away. As she drowned in his arousal and was buoyed by his acceptance, warm emotion flooded her body. With each thrust of his cock, Tina arched her hips toward his and grabbed at his back, desperate to be closer, starving for more. Her pussy gripped him when he pulled away, calling him back, greedy for the friction that sent sensation rioting through her, hurtling her to the edge. Within seconds, she was falling, body quaking, muscles spasming, as a delicious explosion rocked her body and tore a scream from her throat.

It rocked Johnny, too, ripping a guttural grunt from his chest.

His hands were no longer on her face. He was no longer looking at tears that had long dried. Instead, his head hung over her shoulder, his breath blasted her neck with each ragged pant, his hips slapped against hers with each frenzied thrust, until he stilled and trembled, and joined her over the edge.

10

Johnny rolled off of Tina and dropped onto his back, still panting, still trembling. He stared at the ceiling, feeling dazed and disoriented, wallowing in the aftershocks of the orgasm still rolling through him.

Nothing had gone as he'd expected.

He'd made—and watched—a woman cry during sex. The epitome of unsexy; a surefire mood-killer.

Instead, something similar—but not quite the same—to that euphoric rush he got when he put on a great show or had a good workout had settled in his chest and which, despite being non-sexual, had caused his cock to grow harder.

He'd looked into her tear-filled eyes and, instead of seeing cock-hardening lust, saw something complicated reflected back at him. Something that was adoring instead of lustful, soft instead of raw— something that should have caused an equally-soft dick.

Something that should not have made his chest

expand as if he'd won a competition.

Something that should not have made him want to caress her more or pump harder or do whatever it took to make her happy and keep her looking at him like that.

Nothing in the whole experience should have broken his past record for Best Orgasm of His Life by a landslide.

Johnny slid a hand through his hair, as if the simple act could erase his confusion and restore his equilibrium.

Tina slid her hand up his chest as she sidled up to him, head resting against his chest and leg thrown over his hips, her thigh grazing his balls. Her palm explored his pecs. Her fingertips leisurely traced his areola. Her body was relaxed as if she had all the time in the world and was settling in for the night.

Which he'd known would be the case when he'd come over. He knew she wasn't the hit-it-and-quit-it kind. In fact, he hadn't even considered leaving, since he'd been focused on doing everything right.

No, he'd been prepared to hang around. He'd planned to give her toe-curling sex, after which they'd fall immediately asleep and, ego-restored, he'd leave in the morning, guilty-conscience-free.

Instead, they were lying in her bed, doing nothing.

Her head, resting on his arm, turned toward his chest. Her lips kissed the underside of his pec.

His fingertips stroked her arm.

Instead of getting the ball rolling for another bout of sex, he was lying still, letting nothing happen, doing the C-word:

Cuddling.

Johnny couldn't remember when he'd last done

that, not even when he was married. Especially not then. On the rare occasions when Marta had wanted sex, she'd rolled over to her side of the bed once it was over.

Tina's hand trailed over his abs.

He and Marta hadn't touched.

Tina's fingertip slipped to his groin.

He and Marta hadn't caressed.

His skin rippled. His cock twitched.

"You never answered my question."

He and Marta hadn't talked.

"If you keep doing that, I still won't," he said.

He and Marta hadn't teased.

She laughed, her throaty chuckle vibrating against his chest and strumming his cock. "What? You can't feel and talk at the same time?" Her hand slipped lower, teasing the light dusting of hair that now grew—since he was no longer dancing and no longer waxed—in a straight line that led directly to his cock.

But worse than the doing—cuddling, touching, caressing, talking, teasing—was the liking. For the first time he could remember, he *liked* all of it and he *wanted* to stay.

Panic spasmed in his chest. Adrenaline leaked into his veins, flooding his system, giving him the shakes. The urge to flee settled in his legs.

It felt like one of his episodes coming on.

Oh, fuck. Not here, not now!

"Okay. I'll stop." Laughter still threaded her words. She moved her hand back to his abs.

He inhaled deeply and held his breath, waiting for the flashback to hit him. But it didn't. He exhaled, willing his body to relax and his panic to subside. It did—slightly.

Tina drew circles against his skin, seemingly having forgotten her question. "That was fantastic."

He liked the wonder in her voice. "Yeah." He took another deep breath.

"Even better than the first time—and I thought that was wonderful."

Again, he let the air out slowly. He had thought so. But he liked that she had, too. "Yeah."

Can't you say anything else?

Not right now.

As he inhaled and exhaled again and the flashbacks remained absent and the thrum of panic settled into a hum of discomfort, it hit him: This was not going to trigger a flashback to the past. He was locked in the moment, doing things he hadn't done before, feeling things he didn't know how to handle.

So what was he going to do about it?

You need to deal with your shit, J.

If he was going to stay the night, he had no choice.

He took another calming breath and turned his attention outward, concentrating on Tina. For the first time, he wasn't using the focus as a distraction from his thoughts but because he really did want to focus on her.

Another tremor of panic rippled through him.

Another urge to get up and go flickered through him.

He took another deep breath.

He was staying. He was interested. He would try to do this thing tonight, despite the discomfort.

Tina's hands stilled. "About what you did . . . you know, touching my face? I'm so used to people reacting negatively or treating me differently."

Her masked hurt made him want to punch

something—or rather, the someones who put it there.

"But you haven't. And tonight . . ." She paused. ". . . you made me feel whole and normal and beautiful."

The tremble in her voice made his chest tighten—and his cock harden.

"You *are* whole and normal and beautiful." The words sounded gruff.

She looked up at him and smiled, as if finally accepting his words. Gratitude and admiration, mixed with something soft, seemed to shine in her eyes. "I can't tell you how much that means."

Her look seemed adoring, like he had done a great thing or was a hero or something. Only one other woman had ever looked at him like that, and she had died when he was fourteen.

Something seemed to shift in his chest, overwhelming him with some feeling that he couldn't name, let alone express.

It was too much. A wave of panic rolled over him.

He turned to his side. He got on his knees and straddled her thighs, then reached into the nightstand and grabbed another condom. After putting it on, he pulled her on top of him. "Obviously, you need me to show you."

"You just want to see me cry again."

No, I just want you to keep looking at me like that.

"How'd you guess?" Then he drew her head down to his. As their lips touched, humor fled and heat sped through his body.

Her tongue met his, gently exploring before growing demanding.

Johnny was accustomed to leading, to being in control, but it aroused him to let Tina set the pace.

She kissed him like she couldn't get enough. Her hands roamed his body, massaging and caressing, stopping here, exploring there as if she wanted to touch every part of him and would never tire of touching him. She moved against his body as if savoring every stroke. Every touch, every look, seemed laced with a sense of wonder, making sex feel new and fresh.

Which affected him like the strongest aphrodisiac.

With a simple touch, she made him hot.

When she buried him inside her, she took him seconds away from coming.

And when she pumped her hips against him, taking his cock deep within her, clenching and releasing, all the while staring at him with eyes glazed with desire and pleasure, begging him for what he could give her—

Johnny gripped her hips, held her ass, and raised his hips, burying himself as deep as he could, while his cock throbbed, emptying within her.

As the last tremors of his orgasm faded and Tina collapsed on top of him, the feeling he hadn't been able to name or express came to him: Tina made him feel like a man, instead of a shell of one.

~ ~ ~ ~

Tina opened her eyes, awakened by something but not sure what. Her head felt a bit fuzzy, like it always did after drinking wine, even a single glass.

Did I drink wine last night?

The question flickered through her mind before the realization that wine was the least memorable thing she'd done last night.

Johnny.

She smiled.

She turned to her right and there he was, on his back, one arm flung out to the side, the other one slung across his forehead.

Like she'd told him, it had been wonderful. But she hadn't shared the fact that it had been the most wonderful experience of her life—well, the second most, since giving birth to Brianna was the first. Just thinking about how he had caressed her face and looked at her—really *seeing* her—and, instead of being repelled, his desire had increased, nearly brought tears to her eyes. Again.

And then there was the sex.

She let her eyes rove his body, taking in the brawny chest that she had stroked and rubbed and braced herself against as she rode him.

Rode him.

Like a horse or a bull. That analogy was spot on because when she'd gripped his hips with her thighs and bounced up and down, it had felt like riding. And she had felt like a champion rider, yipping and yee-hawing her way to victory.

Her face warmed at the memory. What would he think of her in the bright daylight? What would—

A door opened downstairs. The low murmur of voices, followed by a childish giggle, greeted her ears.

It was Brianna. Tina's smile grew wider. What wo—

Brianna!

Tina yelped and glanced at the clock. 10:48. She never slept this late.

She'd never had a reason to.

Oh my God. Brianna's home! How am I going to explain this? How am I—

Tina jumped out of bed, bent down, and scooped

up Johnny's clothes—shirt, briefs, pants—then turned back to the bed. Leaning down, she nudged him gently, but insistently. "Johnny."

"Hmmm?" he said, still sleep.

She shook him, and once again, softly called his name.

His eyes drifted open. He blinked a few times as if trying to remember where he was, before his gaze settled on her. "Hey."

"Hi. I'm really sorry but you have to get up. Brianna and my mom just got home."

She held his clothes out to him.

"Sure." He sat up, ran a hand through his hair, then over his eyes.

Tina set the clothes on the bed, then raced to the closet and grabbed a pair of jeans and a t-shirt, dressing in record time. "This is so rude, and I'm so, so sorry, but you—"

She turned and stopped in mid-sentence at the sight of Johnny standing by the bed, his back to her, buck naked, putting his pants on. His sculpted body was even more perfect, more beautiful in the light.

He turned toward her, zipping up his pants.

Her gaze darted to his face.

He raised a brow. "But I . . .?"

She remembered her train of thought. "But you have to go."

He walked to a window, pulled back the drape with a fingertip and looked out, before returning his attention to her. "Should I just climb out the window?"

Tina's gaze darted to the window, then back at him. Relief whizzed through her . . .

"That would be great."

His lips twitched.

. . . until she remembered the dense privet hedges right outside. Until she noticed the sarcastic undercurrent running through his words. Until she realized how ridiculous she was being for even thinking it.

"Oh. No." She'd think of something. At a minimum, she'd go downstairs and announce him to lessen the shock. "Just wait here."

She turned and walked toward the door.

The door opened. "Mommy, Grandma got me the doll I . . ." Brianna stopped abruptly, her mouth hanging open, her eyes glued to Johnny.

The blood rushed to Tina's face. She whipped her head around to Johnny, relieved to see him sitting on the bed, putting on his shoes, fully clothed other than his unbuttoned shirt hanging open.

If Brianna had come mere minutes earlier . . .

"Whoa . . ." Brianna breathed.

Tina tamped down her embarrassment and summoned her Stern Mommy Face. "Brianna, go back downstairs, please."

Brianna ignored her, having only eyes for Johnny. "Who are you?"

"Johnny Guerra. And you must be Brianna." He gave her his half-smile.

"Yeah." Brianna looked starstruck. "Are you my new uncle?"

"Uncle?" said Johnny.

"Brianna!" said Tina.

Trance broken, Brianna giggled, shot Tina a big grin, and turned around. She skipped down the hall. "Wait 'til I tell Missy."

Tina turned back to Johnny, both cheeks warm.

"Uh, 'uncle' is what some of the other moms call the men they bring home. I'm sorry."

Tucking in his shirt, he walked toward her. "It's okay. Cute kid."

"Thanks." Tina took a deep breath. "Well, let's go downstairs."

As they entered the kitchen, Tina said, "Mom, this is Johnny. Johnny, this is my mom, Frances, and, well, you already met Brianna."

Johnny gave his sexy smile. "Hi. Nice to meet you both."

Brianna looked up from where she'd been playing with a doll, once again staring at Johnny, strangely subdued after her dramatic entrance upstairs. "Hi."

Tina's mom looked at Johnny and smiled as if strange, gorgeous men came out of Tina's bedroom every day. "Nice to meet you too, Johnny. I was just making some coffee. Would you like some?"

"No, thank you. I need to get going."

"I got a new doll," Brianna said abruptly, her tone slightly challenging, her gaze directed at Johnny. She turned the face around so he could see. It was the one Brianna had talked about months ago. The one with the strawberry birthmark covering her eye and part of her forehead.

"She's pretty," said Johnny.

"Like my mom," said Brianna, chin raised, eyes sparkling, like a young cub defending a lioness.

"Nah." Johnny's gaze drifted to Tina. His eyes roved her face, lingering for the briefest moment on her birthmark, before returning to Brianna. He gave her what Tina termed his "Johnny smile," the one that she imagined charmed any and all women into giving him what he wanted.

Including Tina.

"Your mom's prettier." He winked.

Brianna laughed, the protective lioness replaced by a nine-year-old girl.

Including Brianna.

Goodbyes were exchanged and Tina walked Johnny to the door, then paused awkwardly. "Tha—"

"Do *not* thank me."

"Okay." She bit her lip.

His gaze dropped to her mouth and his eyes darkened, making her think he wanted to kiss her. Which was not going to happen with her family mere feet away, but that didn't stop her lips from parting in invitation or her heart from racing in anticipation.

He returned his gaze, all hot and smoky, to hers. "I'll call you," he said and was gone.

Tina closed the door and nearly fell against it. Did he really plan to call her? Or was it just a line that guys said when they left?

She'd thought their night of pool and sex was a one-time thing.

She'd convinced herself that last night would be the last time she'd see him.

Each time, she had made herself stay in the moment, enjoying the experience for the blessing it was, grateful for a spectacular experience she'd never, ever expected to have, one she'd be able to cherish and reflect on and relive for the rest of her life. Not once had she dared let herself imagine that it was more than a fling. Not once had she counted on seeing him again, though she had wanted it.

But with the words *I'll call you* and the hot look blazing in his eyes—a look that seemed to say he wanted more—Tina couldn't prevent the flicker of hope that he might indeed call.

Do not go there. Keep taking it as it comes, if it comes, expecting nothing lasting, enjoying the moment.

Though she chanted those words in her mind all the way to the kitchen and told herself the happiness buzzing through her body was solely from last night, she couldn't stop herself from softly singing the chorus line from Carrie Underwood's song, *See You Again.*

But she did resist the urge to skip back to the kitchen. Barely.

Brianna, hunched over the iPad, didn't look up. But her mother, sipping her coffee and doing nothing, as if waiting for Tina, did. She looked amused.

"Someone's happy," said Frances.

"I am. It's Saturday, it's sunny, and I don't have to work today." She grabbed a cup and swooped over to the coffee pot.

"Umm-hmm," said Frances. That one sound let Tina know she wasn't fooled.

Tina poured coffee and added cream and sugar before turning to her mother. "So, what did you and Brianna do last night?"

"Well, Brianna wanted me to watch *Matilda* with her. Again." She sighed.

Tina laughed. For some reason—one that started with a J—she felt like grinning and laughing about everything today. "Better you than me." Tina took a sip of coffee.

"Yes. But fortunately, her doll had arrived, so she wanted to play with that all night instead. Remind me to kiss the postman."

Still smiling, Tina picked up the doll. She

smoothed her fingers over the bright red splotches—made all the brighter by the pale flesh-colored plastic—that circled the doll's right eye and half of her forehead, with a few additional splotches spilling onto her nose, upper lip, and cheek. Despite the blemish, her big eyes, innocent expression, and pink dress made her look cute. Or maybe she looked cute because of the blemish, for the more Tina stared, the more the reddish-pink colorations looked like an artfully applied half-mask, adding a bit of mystery and allure that contributed to her cuteness.

Is this what I look like? To those who know me or love me, those who are able to see beyond the blemish. Is that what they see?

Maybe her mother was right. Maybe Brianna was right. Maybe Johnny was right. Maybe she *was* pretty to some people.

"So, what did *you* do last night?"

Tina's eyes darted to her mother's—and the amusement twinkling there—and blushed.

"Obviously, you didn't eat."

"Oh, the food." For the first time she remembered, and for the first time she noticed that the lamb she'd removed from the oven was no longer on the counter. She reached for the microwave to check the potatoes.

"I took care of it."

"Mom!" exclaimed Brianna.

Tina looked at Brianna, who was staring at something on her iPad.

"Johnny's a dancer! Did you know he's a dancer?"

Tina's blood fled her face, taking the blush with it. "What are you looking at?" Images of a nearly-naked Johnny flashed through her mind as she rushed over to Brianna. Relief flooded her at what appeared to be a publicity shot of a bare-chested, muscle-bound Johnny wearing his I-want-you-now stare. She made a mental note to see if parental control settings could be used to block Internet access to Johnny.

"He can help me with my dance routine!"

"No, he is not going to help you with your dance routine."

"Mom, can you ask him?"

"Honey, I don't know Johnny that well."

"Seems to me like you know him pretty well," her mother muttered.

Tina shot her mother a glare.

Frances grinned.

"Well, can I ask him?"

"No. He's very busy." She smoothed Brianna's hair. "I'll help you."

Brianna rolled her eyes. "You can't dance."

"But I know good dancing when I see it." She kissed the top of Brianna's head. "And *you* are a very good dancer."

The doorbell rang.

Dance routines and hunky dancers forgotten, Brianna squirmed away and grabbed her doll. "That's Missy. I told her about my doll and she's coming over to see it."

"I'll go with her to the door," said her mother.

Seconds later, girlish voices and giggling were heard in the hallway and up the stairs, ending with the sound of a door closing.

Frances returned to the kitchen. "So, now that Brianna's gone, are you going to tell me how you met that gorgeous man?"

She'd known her mother was going to ask. Tina

thought she was prepared. But now that she'd been asked, Tina didn't know what to say.

I was fondling his photos and he caught me?

Perhaps a generic version would be better. "Weeks ago, I started watering the plants in his office. And he was there late one night and we got to talking."

"He seems nice."

"Yeah."

"And good-looking."

"Yeah."

"He seems to like you."

Tina shrugged. "We're becoming good . . . friends."

Her mother laughed. "That man does not think of you as a *friend*."

Tina's lighthearted mood dissolved. She looked at the vase of sunflowers, then fiddled with the iPad cover, still not looking at her mom. "But I'm trying to think of him as a friend, Mom."

"Why?"

"Partly because I don't know if I'll even hear from him again."

"And the other part?"

Tina paused, struggling to put her doubts and fears about Johnny into words. "I don't know."

Her mother remained silent then said softly, "He's not David, Tina."

Tina traced the groove in the leather with her finger. "I know. But . . ."

"But what?"

"I could never figure out why men couldn't see me, couldn't look beyond my face and see *me*." She shrugged. "And then I meet this beautiful man who seems to, and . . . I can't totally believe it's true. Or I don't want to believe it's true, because I'm scared."

Tina felt her mother step forward seconds before feeling Frances's arm around her. Frances squeezed her shoulders and bent her head forward, planting a kiss on Tina's head just as Tina had done to Brianna.

"Teeny, men couldn't see you because you didn't let them. The few that tried, you forced them away." She stroked Tina's hair. "Maybe things will work out, maybe they won't. Maybe you'll be deliriously happy or maybe he'll break your heart. But one thing is for sure: He sees you. But do you see him?"

Tina finally looked at her mother, at the love in her eyes. "Of course."

Frances shook her head. "No. You look at his beautiful face, just as others have looked at yours. And just as others have done to you, you don't see *him*."

Tina pondered what she thought about Johnny, how all of her ideas and notions about who he was or how he felt were based on her ideas of "He's beautiful so he must be this" or "He's beautiful so he must feel that." She looked at his face but didn't look any further. She had challenged him to let her see the *real* him, but then she'd dismissed everything that didn't fit the image of who she thought he was.

Her mother was right.

She was doing the same thing to Johnny that others did to her.

Her stomach clenched. A lump formed in her throat.

She wrapped her arms around her mother and rested her head on Frances's breast and, for the second time in twenty-four hours, Tina cried.

11

I'll call you.

Johnny couldn't believe he'd uttered the words that he never said to women and that he hadn't needed to say to Tina. He'd done everything right—performed better sexually, managed to string coherent sentences together, and left her seemingly satisfied and happy— just as he'd promised himself. Thus, his redo had been successful, he'd redeemed himself from the pool sex fiasco, and he was free to walk away with a kiss and a smile and a clear conscience.

But he hadn't.

Not even after being asked to sneak out of a window, then being caught in Tina's bed by her young daughter, then having to pretend like nothing happened with Tina's mother. He hadn't experienced that much drama since high school.

And yet he'd still said, "I'll call you." Which he didn't regret because he *did* want to call her.

And therein lay the real reason for his surprise.

Johnny shook his head and entered his office.

"This is a first," said Brandon. "Me beating *you* into the office for our little Saturday afternoon *tête-à-tête*."

"Something came up."

"Hmmm. Would that 'something' happen to be a pretty brunette pool aficionado?"

Johnny ignored the question. "Did you follow up on the tiered seats?"

"Okay. That means 'Yes, she was the something.' And to answer *your* question, yes, I did and they are scheduled for delivery next month, on the 27th."

"Good. And the lighting and sound system—Club Boudoir's good with that?"

"Yes. Now, back to the original topic. She must really be 'something.' You've never brought anyone to the practice room, let alone our pool game."

"You invited her."

"Because I liked her. But since you could have charmingly uninvited her but didn't, methinks that you like her, too."

So I'm discovering.

"You know I don't pry into your business."

"You always pry into my business, Brandon."

"No, I always *try* to pry into your business."

"What is this about?"

Brandon dropped all pretense of joking. "You seem to be doing good. No episodes."

Johnny hadn't thought about that, but, yeah—other than the mini-episode triggered by Tina's husband/father dance request, there hadn't been any. It was too soon to tell if that would last but, so far, Brandon was right.

"You seem more relaxed."

He felt more relaxed.

"So if it's because of her, I just wanted to say great, go for it. You haven't given anyone a chance since, well, you know."

Yeah, he knew. But he didn't want to think about that.

"I'm just saying, a good woman can make all the difference."

Johnny didn't know what having a good woman was like. But then again, he didn't know what being a good man was like, either. Unlike Brandon who, despite his messed-up marriage and feigned nonchalance about it, had experienced both—and wanted to again.

But Johnny didn't want to think about that, either. At least not as it applied to him.

"Just don't make my mistakes. Don't fuck this up, J."

Johnny didn't know what the 'this' was with Tina or if he was up for the good woman/good man thing. All he knew was he didn't want to think about things or analyze them or, as his therapist had said, 'process' how he was feeling.

The only thing he knew was that he wanted to keep seeing Tina until he didn't want to see her anymore.

Brandon cleared his throat. "So, are you done asking me for advice?"

Johnny's lips quirked. "Yeah."

"Good. Because I have an idea for a new show." Brandon jumped up from the chair. He raised his arms, fingers forming a half-square, and spread them as if seeing a marquee. "Kind of an old-meets-new thing, a tribute to classic movies. We have snippets from well-known movies playing on big screens in the background with the guys dancing in front."

Relieved to be discussing business, Johnny leaned back in his chair. "I like the concept."

Brandon paced the floor, totally engrossed, gesturing passionately with his hands while he talked. All traces of relationship woes were forgotten. "Like the black and white *Tarzan* movies, while we dance in loin cloth. Or *Cyrano de Bergerac* and the guys are in Cavalier costumes and brandishing swords. Each set is a different movie."

"Those sets sound expensive."

"We'd only need two different sets, which would change during the break, if we group movies around themes."

Johnny nodded. "It could work. Get me details and costs and we'll see."

"*Yessss.*" Brandon fisted his hand, bent his elbow, and jerked his arm downward. "I'm on it."

"Be 'on it' on Monday. I need you at the show tonight to keep an eye on that new guy, Tim."

Brandon walked to the door. "Okay."

"And go home to your wife."

"Sure. And you should go back to your new woman." Brandon winked and left.

Your new woman.

Johnny frowned. He wanted to see Tina, but calling her his woman was going too far.

Well, do you want someone else to fuck her?

Hell, no. Johnny didn't even like the word 'fuck' and her name, without his, in the same sentence.

Then, there you have it. She's your new woman.

He pushed the thought from his mind and looked at his calendar, then picked up his cell to call—

Your new woman

—*Tina*, as promised.

"Hello, Johnny?"

The childish voice on the line took Johnny by surprise. "Brianna?"

"Yes. I answered the phone to tell you Mom's in the shower."

"Okay. Please ask her to call me."

"I will. But, really, I wanted to call you but Mommy wouldn't let me."

Another surprise. What could the kid want with him?

"See, I have this dance performance at my school and I have to win it but I need help and Mommy can't help me because she's a really bad dancer so since I saw on YouTube that you're a really good dancer—"

Johnny blanched. "You saw one of my videos on YouTube?"

"No. I was going to but Mommy blocked it." Brianna's tone implied that a grave injustice had been done.

Thank God.

"But I saw that you had like, a bazillion views, so I figured you must be a good dancer. So, will you help me?"

A wave of panic surfaced. He hadn't signed up for this. He was just getting used to the idea of seeing a woman more than a couple nights. But hanging out with her kid? This was too much. Johnny took a deep calming breath. "Uh, no. Sorry, Brianna. I can't."

"Why not?"

He exhaled fully.

Because you're afraid. Buck-buck-buck-buckbuck.

"Because I don't do the kind of dance you need."

He inhaled.

"Yes, you do."

He exhaled, feeling more relaxed.

"You do exactly the kind of dance I need. The website said you're an *exotic* dancer."

Johnny choked.

"And I need something exotic so I can win for sure."

Oh, so that's what she meant by 'exotic.' "Sorry. I'm not the guy for you."

She remained silent.

Johnny shifted in his chair, anxious to get off the phone, despite the flicker of guilt, despite feeling like the Grinch Who Stole Christmas. "Well, have your mom—"

A soft mewl, followed by a faint hiccup-filled sob, interrupted him.

Ahh, shit. She was crying. His panic grew, clenching his stomach. "Look, I'm sure you'll think of something."

The sobs became louder.

Tension wound through Johnny's chest, tightening around his lungs, trapping his breath. What the fuck was he supposed to do now?

"But I *need* you to help." It was a tear-filled wail that pierced his panic, tugging at something inside of him. "Because I have to win because the winner gets $250 and I need the money."

Johnny frowned. "Does your mom have money problems?"

"No. *I* have money problems. I've been saving my allowance and sometimes my lunch money, when I'm not hungry." She paused and lowered her voice to a watery whisper. "I'm saving money for Mommy's face operation so she will feel happy and beautiful and normal and then I can have a daddy like my friend Missy does."

Johnny's chest felt odd again. That heavy, tight sensation was not due to panic, because panic was still bunkered down in his stomach.

He exhaled noisily.

The tightness remained.

Her sobs had returned to soft hiccup sounds.

Think of something. Make her stop. Make her feel better.

Johnny made a slow, downward patting motion with his hand, though whether it was to calm her or him he wasn't sure. "Okay, okay, le—"

"Oh, thank you, thank you!"

"What?"

Her unhappy sobs turned into happy ones. "I knew you'd do it!"

I didn't say I'd do it! I was gonna say 'Let's calm down.'

"You need to tell Mommy so she'll say it's okay. But you can't tell her about the money or the face operation. That's a surprise."

"Wait—"

"Mom! Johnny needs to tell you something!"

What!

He heard Tina's muffled voice in the background.

"She'll be here in a minute."

Panic bubbled up from its nap, spilling out from his stomach and entering his bloodstream. His breathing quickened. His mind raced, scrambling to say something to set the kid straight, to let her know once and for all that he was not the right person to give her lessons.

Maybe he could find someone else. Maybe—

An idea sparked. Yes. Brandon—family man

Brandon. He could do it.

But something didn't sit right with Johnny about that solution, either.

"Here she is. And Johnny?"

"Uh, yeah?"

"Thank you." Two little words. They sounded so sincere, so heartfelt. As if he were Santa Claus and had just given her the thing she wanted most in the whole world.

Johnny felt that heavy thing wrap itself around his chest again. It wasn't a painful sensation. It wasn't unpleasant. Actually, it was kind of good. Kind of like when his muscles trembled and endorphins flooded his body after a good workout or a long run, giving him that runner's high.

Tina's muffled voice in the distance brought him back to the present. "Brianna, were you crying?"

"Yep. But they were happy tears. Here's Johnny."

"Hi, Johnny."

"Hey."

"How are you?"

Confused. Wondering what the fuck I'm doing.

"Good. You?"

"I'm good," Tina said. "What was that all about?"

"We were talking about her dance."

"Oh, no. Did she ask you for help?"

Now, how was he supposed to answer that? If he said yes, he'd get the kid in trouble. If he said no, he'd be lying, which Johnny prided himself on never doing to women, even if *this* lie was for a good reason.

Tina made the decision for him. "Brianna, did you ask Johnny to help you with your dance?"

He heard Brianna's resigned, here-comes-the-hanging, "Yes."

"You, young lady, are grounded. Which we will discuss after I get off the phone. I'm so sorry, Johnny," Tina said. "I told her not to ask you that."

I'm saving money for Mommy's face operation so she will feel happy and beautiful and normal and then I can have a daddy like my friend Missy does.

Here it was, his last chance to get out of it, to pass the buck to Brandon.

But something didn't seem right about passing the buck to Brandon. For one thing, Johnny didn't pass his problems on to others. He dealt—or didn't deal—with them himself. But more importantly, something about Brianna's plea got him.

I'm gonna get this cleft palate fixed when I get out of here.

It reminded him of his friend Dwayne at the Home who'd planned to use his money the same way—until he'd hooked up with a gang who told him his lip made him look tough.

"It's okay." Johnny took a deep breath, attempting to push out the last bit of panic floating around in his gut. "I told her I'd do it."

"What?"

What! You had an out!

"I don't think—" said Tina.

"Right. Don't think." Johnny's voice became persuasive. For both of them. "It's important to her."

She paused then said, "Why are you doing this?"

Because I like you. "Because she seems like a good kid."

Getting involved with her kid goes a little beyond 'like.'

He was not getting involved with Brianna. He was only helping her. Like he hadn't been able to help Dwayne, who'd been gunned down in a drive-by. "I teach dance at the Y. It's no big deal. One lesson is all

144

it will take."

"Please, Mom. Pleeeease," he heard Brianna say in the background.

Tina's pause was even longer before she finally said, "Okay. But only this one time."

With that, the lingering traces of Johnny's discomfort began to fade. He and Tina were on the same page. It was a one-time thing, with no additional expectations.

"Cool. See you both Friday at seven, at Hot Dreams?"

"That's fine." Another pause. "Thank you." Whispery threads of you're-like-Santa-Claus laced her words, just as they'd done to Brianna's.

And he liked that.

But as he hung up the phone, Johnny couldn't help thinking again, *What the fuck am I doing?*

12

Johnny heard the indistinct sound of Brianna's chatter and Tina's response as they approached the dance studio. Surprisingly, his panic hadn't returned. Nor had his discomfort. On a much smaller scale, his initial feelings about this lesson were like when he'd made the decision to expand Hot Dreams from merely a strip-o-gram service to a male entertainment company. He'd panicked over the idea, fearing it was too soon to grow the business, that he'd made a mistake and would fail. But once he'd made the decision to do it, the panic subsided. Deciding to do something always took more emotional energy than doing it.

Thus, decision made, he was calm, in control, and prepared for the lesson.

Until Tina and Brianna arrived.

He was not prepared for the rush of lust that hit him as Tina stood in the doorway, wearing a sleeveless, form-fitting dress with big pastel-colored flowers, reminiscent of Betty in *Mad Men*. A hesitant smile curved her lips. Her hand rested lightly on Brianna's shoulder.

All of which made for a pretty pose, perhaps worthy of a Norman Rockwell painting, but it should not have inspired lust.

And yet his heart pounded and heat rushed to his groin as if she were standing alone and naked, staring at him with that glazed look that said she wanted him right now, right there, any way.

"This is just like my ballet classroom," Brianna said, breaking his unexpected trance. She ran to the windows and stared outside.

"Hi," Johnny said to Tina.

"Hi," she said back. The arm that no longer embraced Brianna clutched the purse strap looped over her shoulder. She remained unmoving, standing in the doorway as if unsure whether to stay or take Brianna and flee.

Johnny fought the urge to go to her, take her arm and guide her forward, maybe planting a chaste kiss on her cheek while whispering unchaste words in her ear. Instead, he extended his hand, palm up, in a come-in motion.

She did.

"Except this room is way cooler," said Brianna.

His gaze, surprisingly reluctant, moved from Tina to Brianna.

"Do you dance here?"

"No. The men who work for me do."

Brianna turned to him with a frown. "Why don't you dance here?"

Johnny smiled. Like mother, like daughter. He looked at Tina to see if she noticed that her daughter was asking the same question she'd asked in the same room.

Her faint smile told him she had.

"Because I don't dance anymore." He went to the iPod before Brianna could ask another question. "Do you have a song in mind?"

"Yes. I want *All About That Bass*. Do you have that?"

"Yeah." He shuffled through the songs until he came to it. "So, do you know what you want to do?"

"Sorta. I want to do something exotic."

Johnny's lips twitched. "Yeah, I got that."

"So I was thinking, during that first part of the song that she sings over and over again?"

"The refrain."

"Yeah, that. The refrain. I could do some ballet moves because I'm good at ballet and then you can teach me some hip-hop moves for the other parts." She scrunched up her face in concentration. "Kinda like Michael Jackson." She moved her shoulders then thrust her non-existent hips front-to-back in a non-kid-friendly way.

"Uh, let's skip the hip part," Johnny said.

"Oh, no. You are *not* doing that," Tina said.

They both spoke at the same time.

Johnny glanced at Tina. With her eyebrows raised, head tilted in Brianna's direction, lips pursed, her expression said she meant business. Her hands were now on her hips. Her index finger tapped against her waist, as if ticking off the seconds as she waited for Brianna's acquiescence. Authority radiated from her, like a commanding officer waiting for his underlings to follow his orders. Or a Dominatrix awaiting her sub's obeyance to her command.

You've been a naughty boy, Johnny.

Yeah, like that. He could imagine Tina standing over him, one hand on her hip, one of those feather duster things in the other hand and—

What the fuck? This is not the time for that.

"But, Moooom."

Johnny jerked his attention back to Brianna.

"How about if we do this?" Johnny said, distracting Brianna from mutiny and himself from BDSM fantasies he never knew he had. He moved his hips non-suggestively from side-to-side. "It's a nice transition from being on your tippy toes—"

"It's not tippy toes. It's *en pointe.*" Brianna's green eyes, miniature versions of her mother's, glistened with suppressed annoyance, as if she were instructing a dimwit student.

Johnny smiled. Teaching Brianna really wasn't that different than teaching the boys at the YMCA. They'd worn similar expressions of outrage when he'd told them to lie on their back and do hip roll exercises, claiming it was for sissies. "Right. When you're *en pointe . . .*" Straightening his back, raising his chin to an exaggerated height, and donning his most snobbish look, he stood on his tippy toes and shifted from foot to foot in place.

Brianna giggled.

He looked down his nose at her and in a French dialect that sounded more like Ms. Piggy with a bad British accent, said, "Voo do not loff."

Brianna covered her mouth to hide her giggle.

"As I was saying, as you start coming off *pointe,* begin wiggling your hips from side-to-side."

She mimicked his actions.

"Then, when you're completely on your feet, do this." He shifted to the right, then shifted to the left, putting his hands on his hips.

She did the same thing.

"Not bad. Ready for music?"

"Yeah."

"Okay. Face the mirror."

With that, his mind zoomed back to Tina and the time when he'd said those same words to her in front of this same mirror.

"Face the mirror," he'd said.

"I don't . . . like mirrors," she'd said.

When he'd placed his hands on her shoulders and turned her around, the pads of his fingers resting against her collarbone had itched to trace it. To inch forward before moving downward, the palms of his hands grazing her breasts, before cupping and squeezing them.

But when he'd told her she wouldn't be looking at herself, uncertainty had given way to wonder, then her eyes had darkened at the realization that she'd be looking at him. He'd had to turn away before his hands acted on the fantasies roaming his mind.

He caught Tina's gaze in the glass.

Like then, her eyes were sultry and hot.

Like then, Johnny had to turn away.

"Now what?" Brianna, eagerly waiting in front of the glass, brought him back.

Johnny pressed play and Megan Trainor's Southern-tinged voice filled the room.

He did the moves and Brianna followed. Then he introduced a few new ones. She stumbled a bit but kept trying.

Once again, Johnny looked at Tina.

Once again, he was shocked by her expression.

But this time what stunned him was the depth of

love that seemed to shine from her eyes as she watched her daughter. A pain stabbed his chest at the memory of Marta, whose indifference toward their child had quickly turned to resentment and hate.

Would she have felt about Junior the way Tina felt about Brianna, if he'd been more attentive?

Like you are with Tina?

He pushed the thoughts of Marta and Tina away.

"How was that?"

Johnny jerked his attention back to Brianna, realizing he'd been dancing on automatic pilot. "Let's do it one more time."

After about fifteen minutes, she had it down.

He was impressed. "Good. I think you're ready to do it alone."

He moved out of the way and cued the song.

Brianna started again, this time singing along. Her voice was surprisingly strong, without that high-pitched kid sound that many young girls had. He was even more impressed.

"Great job," he said, when she was finished. "I think you're going to win that contest."

She grinned, beaming, before turning to her mom. "Did you see me?"

Tina was also beaming, like the proud mom she should be.

Once again, Marta's resentment flickered through his mind.

He pushed it away.

"Yes, honey. You were wonderful."

"Now, I want to do something else that I don't want you to see until the night of the show. So can you leave for about ten minutes?"

Tina's smile faded. She nibbled her lower lip. The

action convinced Johnny that it had, indeed, been worry that he'd glimpsed earlier.

"Mom." This time, Brianna's tone was impatient instead of pleading.

"Okay. But only for ten minutes. And remember what we talked about." Tina's hands went back to her hips. "This is only one time. We may not see Johnny again."

This time, Johnny found nothing sexy about her pose.

This time, there was nothing endearing about her words.

We *may not see Johnny again.*

What the hell did that mean?

"Fine," said Brianna.

Fine? No, everything was not 'fine.'

Tina smiled at Johnny before heading to the door.

Johnny didn't smile back.

Brianna whirled around to him the minute her mother left the room. Her small face was serious and intense as if she were about to reveal world trade secrets. "So here's what I really want to do . . ."

~~~~

As Tina entered Johnny's office with the watering can, she kept seeing Brianna's face, how happy she was, how well she danced. That filled Tina with pride—and it didn't seem to be simply misplaced, biased mother's pride. Brianna had real talent. She could tell even Johnny thought so.

Johnny.

Had she done the right thing, letting Brianna come here? The only reason she'd agreed was because, for some reason, winning this dance competition was extremely important to Brianna. Tina had grounded

Brianna for asking Johnny, but Brianna hadn't complained about her punishment—a week without television, Missy, and going outside. She'd suffered through it with nary a whine, even more proof of the dance competition's importance to her.

She wanted Brianna to be happy, but she didn't want her to get hurt.

Which was why she'd stressed to Brianna before they came—and again during the lesson—that it was only this one time.

We may not see Johnny again.

That statement wasn't just a warning to Brianna. It was also a warning to herself.

Maybe she should just nip whatever this was in the bud now before either she or Brianna got hurt.

As she moved to water the Pothos, Tina's gaze skimmed over the photos. She set the pot down and picked up the one that had started it all with Johnny, thinking how never in a million years did she ever think she'd get to actually experience the "real" him, and how the "real" him was so much better than she could ever have imagined. She loved the way he looked at her and accepted her as a woman in a way she'd never, ever thought possible. She loved the spectacular sex she'd never imagined, and she loved the way he was with Brianna.

Are those the only things you love?

She feared she was actually falling for him. No, she knew she was. And that wasn't a good thing. Because, really, how could this work? He was beautiful and could have—

You look at his beautiful face, just as others have looked at yours. And just as others have done to you, you don't see him.

Her mother was right. Tina had to stop projecting

her own insecurities onto him. But she didn't know if she could. She didn't even know why he was doing all this, why he was with her. It hadn't been important in the beginning, when she'd known it was a game, when it was all about living out a fantasy. Because then, it really was fantasy—fantasy that she'd known was a lie.

Now, it was fantasy that she wanted to believe was reality, a fantasy that would hurt her if she found out it was all a lie.

Like David.

Tina didn't know the rules of dating—or whatever this was she and Johnny were doing. Maybe it was too soon to have any sort of serious conversation of what this was. But, for her own peace of mind, she had to know. Was this part of the game, or was it real?

Or maybe she just needed to get out now, while the hurt of leaving would be less.

With a sigh, Tina set the photo back on the credenza. She should go get Brianna. She took out her cell phone and looked at the time. It had only been five minutes. No, she had to wait. Brianna would be upset but, more importantly, Tina had promised her ten minutes. What difference would another five minutes make?

"Hey, J—"

Tina whirled around with a startled yelp, almost flinging the photo again. What was it about people sneaking up on her in Johnny's office and her penchant for breaking his photos?

"Oh, sorry, Tina. I didn't mean to scare you. I heard someone here and thought it was Johnny."

"That's okay, Brandon. He's in the dance room teaching my daughter, Brianna."

Brandon gaped.

Tina gave him a half-smile. "Yeah, I'm shocked too." *And I'm still wondering if I did the right thing.*

Brandon closed his mouth.

"I've been banished to the office, doing what I do best." She pointed to the watering can.

Brandon regained his composure enough to laugh. "That is not what you do best. How did you learn to play pool like that?"

"My dad." Tina swept a hand toward the frames, using the first thing that came to mind to change the topic. "Do you have photos like these?"

"No, not really. I did in the beginning, when this was all new and exciting."

"It's not exciting, now?"

"No. I'm married."

"You say that like it's the end of the world."

He smiled, though his smile looked strained to Tina. "Nah, it's good." He pointed to the pictures. "Johnny just keeps those for clients and the guys he interviews. The interviewees come in, see those, and think, 'That could be me.'" He grinned again. "I did."

Tina couldn't prevent the flash of happiness she felt that the photos meant nothing to Johnny. Another sign of the emotional danger she was in. Just as her desire to pick Brandon's brain about Johnny was. But that didn't stop her. "So that's how you met him?"

"No. Johnny and I went to high school together. In college, I got into football and he majored in art—"

"Art?"

Brandon smiled. "Yep. Then he stumbled into dancing, liked the money, and realized he wasn't into the 'starving' part of art, so he dropped out almost immediately and started dancing fulltime until . . ." He caught himself, as if he was about to say something he shouldn't. ". . . until he didn't want to dance anymore. He'd started Hot Dreams, started hiring guys to strip, then moved up to shows. When I finished college and my football career was over—I was never good enough for the pros—I started working here, then met my wife at a show, got married, and here I am."

"You seem like a good friend."

Brandon shrugged, as if uncomfortable with the compliment. "We've been through some tough times. Johnny's a good guy."

"Yes, he is."

Tina glanced at the time again. Okay, it had been eleven minutes. Time to get Brianna. Before she could say goodbye to Brandon, she heard the sound of running feet seconds before Brianna appeared.

"Mom, you should have seen . . ." Brianna's mouth dropped open when she saw Brandon, her expression nearly identical to when she'd first seen Johnny. "O M G."

"Hello. You must be Brianna. I'm Brandon." He offered his hand to her for a handshake.

Brianna shook it.

"I hear Johnny gave you dance lessons. He's a horrible dancer. You should have waited for me to teach you." He winked.

"Will you wait for me?" Brianna asked, finally finding her tongue.

"Wait for you?"

"Until I grow up and finish college and become a veterinarian, and then marry me."

Brandon laughed.

Tina rolled her eyes. "On that note, I think it's time for us to go see Grandma. Say goodbye, Brianna."

"Bye," said Brianna.

"Bye, Brandon," said Tina. She turned to Johnny, feeling all gooey and scared and a bit sad inside. She hid it all with a smile. Or so she hoped. "Thank you."

His eyes narrowed slightly.

Oh. Right. He didn't like 'thank you.' "I mean, goodbye." That sounded even worse. Stilted, impersonal, something she would say distractedly to a cashier at the grocery store on her way out.

Goodbye for now, or goodbye forever?

He smiled. Though calling that a smile was like calling the Big Bad Wolf's show of teeth a grin. "Why don't you stop by for dinner after you drop Brianna off?"

13

Standing in front of the door to Johnny's condo, Tina smoothed her dress and puffed her hair. The extra time she'd spent on her appearance instilled a little courage, but she still felt nervous. Mostly because she needed to ask questions she didn't know how to broach. And because Johnny, despite his wolfish smile, had seemed aloof when he'd returned with Brianna to his office.

According to Brianna, who'd chattered nonstop about her dance moves the whole ride home, he'd been great. So maybe it was Tina's imagination. Maybe she was the only one experiencing any discomfort.

She repositioned the box that held a custom-made cake she'd picked up yesterday to thank him for today's lesson.

After straightening her dress one last time, Tina rang the doorbell.

Less than a minute later, Johnny answered, wearing a white terry cloth robe. His hair was wet as if he'd just stepped out of the shower, making Tina's mouth water at the realization that he was probably naked underneath. She could simply walk up to him, untie the belt and slide her hands under the lapels and push the robe off his shoulders, and he would be sinfully naked. They could do it against the wall, which seemed to be the location of choice in a lot of movie sex scenes.

That is, if she hadn't come there to talk.

Riiiight.

Well, to talk *first*.

That is, if Johnny hadn't been making her uncomfortable. Just like the first day in his office, he was staring at her with that dark intense gaze, as if sorting through the private thoughts in her mind, discovering her secrets, while his remained hidden.

"Hi." Tina held out the box to him. "I brought dessert."

He ignored the box. Instead, his eyes traveled her body, lingering on the hint of cleavage peeking out the top of the halter bodice of her dress before dropping to her thighs, which were bare and freshly shaved and extra smooth from her favorite aloe-based body scrub and lotion. His eyes glittered as his gaze returned to hers. "You look like dessert."

Her face warmed. Her breath caught. "I brought the *edible* dessert."

He raised a brow while he took another leisurely tour of her body, his tongue tucked against his upper lip as if in anticipation of tasting something delicious—and that the delicious something was her.

This time, Tina's face warmed in embarrassment, tinged with excitement at the idea.

Just as Johnny reached out to take the box from

her and leaned toward her for what she hoped was a kiss, she heard a voice behind her in the hall.

Johnny moved away.

Disappointment flickered through her.

"I have a delivery for Johnny Guerra."

"That's me."

Money changed hands. Bags were handed to Johnny. As the delivery person left, a delicious aroma wafted under her nose.

"Something smells good."

"I don't cook. But Wild Ginger makes a great coconut lamb dish."

Lamb. The meal she'd cooked for them that they'd never bothered to eat. Tina was touched by his thoughtfulness in seeming to pick something he knew she'd like.

Hands full, he gave her a kiss. A quick nibble. A small taste. A tease that left her yearning for more. His eyes were hooded when he drew back. "Come in."

Tina did, following along behind him, forcing her eyes from his ass, outlined by the cotton, trying to ignore the muscular calves brushing against the hem of the robe. She pushed her lust to the background and focused on her surroundings.

His condo was a trendy converted warehouse loft. One wall was nearly all windows that looked out over Puget Sound, while a mix of different-colored brick—grey, tan, and reddish-brown—covered the remaining walls, framing the glossy nutmeg-colored hardwood floor. The floor plan was open—a long rectangle with living room, office, family room, and kitchen blending together, with only furniture and colorful carpets distinguishing one from the other.

What was most surprising was the décor. Given his contemporary office and stylish clothes, Tina would have taken him for an ultra-modern guy, maybe leather couches and everything in white or black and chrome. Instead, his place was decorated in warm, earthy tones. A comfy chocolate U-shaped couch that looked big enough to seat twelve dominated the living room area, while a massive oak table with matching chairs and antique white seat covers filled the dining space. Colorful rugs in orange, red, and yellow hues and patterns lay under the furnishings, while an eclectic mix of art—from African masks to Native American totem poles to Mexican serapes to moody photographs featuring Seattle's eternal rain and fog and gloom—dotted the room.

The overall effect was homey and inviting and warm . . . words that, when staring at his photo, she would never have expected to use in a sentence with his name.

She was learning that he was so much more than his photos.

"Great place."

"Thanks."

Johnny turned toward the kitchen and placed the food cartons on the caramel-colored granite countertop. She did the same, setting the cake down.

"Can I help with something?"

He handed her a glass of wine when she turned around. "Relax." His voice was soothing. His eyes looked a little warmer.

Was it obvious that she was nervous?

"Have a seat."

She chose to walk around instead, gazing at the

artwork on his walls. She took a sip of wine, smiling at an oil painting featuring ducks wearing yellow raincoats. She took a sip of wine, admiring a rust-colored metal wall hanging of the sun.

Despite numerous sips, the wine increased her nervousness instead of relaxing her. Or maybe it was Johnny's silence. She liked comfortable silence, but this silence felt decidedly *un*comfortable.

She set her useless alcoholic beverage on a coaster resting on an end table and resumed her art walk.

An abstract painting with a bold yellow background caught her eye. She moved closer, taking in the swirling and circling lines in bright colors that filled a black square. The name of the artist stunned her.

She turned toward Johnny. "You painted this?"

Johnny looked up from the food he'd been scraping from a carton. He studied the painting as if he'd forgotten it was there. "Yeah. Years ago. One of the few things I did that was good enough to hang."

Tina turned back to the painting. It was stunning in its simplicity, arresting in its use of colors. "It's beautiful."

"It kinda looks like you."

"What?" Her smile was confused as she stared at the painting. Then she saw it—the pattern of her birthmark.

Uncomfortable with the likening of her blemish to art, yet oddly touched, she brushed the compliment off with a joke. "I bet you say that to all the women." She gave him a teasing smile.

He wasn't smiling. "I don't bring women here."

A thrill rippled through her chest at the implied meaning. But Tina no longer wanted to read meaning into words. She wanted to *know*. Using it as a segue to broach the subject she'd been struggling to bring up, she said, "What does that mean?"

"What do you think it means?" His voice was soft.

She stared at him staring at her. Just like that first day in the office, his gaze in the photos and in person had been shuttered. Then, that look had made her wonder if he ever felt anything, if he ever got any emotional enjoyment out of interactions with those women. Over the past few weeks, she'd seen his eyes lighten and darken with emotion, giving her an even better answer—that he enjoyed being with *her*. Now, since his warm words were at odds with his expressionless gaze, she guessed that he donned his shuttered expression like a mask, using it to hide emotion, not because he felt none.

That knowledge gave her the courage to press for an answer. "I don't know. I only know what I want it to mean. I want *you* to tell *me*."

He stared at her, unmoving, unsmiling. "What did you mean by 'We may not be seeing Johnny again?'"

Something clicked. The aloofness that she'd convinced herself was her imagination. The uncomfortable silence that she'd tried to convince herself was comfortable. Had her suspicions been correct? Could Johnny be annoyed by her reminder to Brianna? A rush of hope rippled through her. "Exactly what I said. I didn't know if you'd be around much longer."

She'd assumed David would be in her life.

She'd assumed Johnny wouldn't.

She didn't want to assume anymore. She wanted to *know*.

"I want you to be around," said Tina.

Something alive flickered behind his mask of unreadability, then was gone.

"I want to see you." The double meaning of her words hit her the minute she said them. The literal meaning—that she wanted to continue getting together, getting to know him—and the one she'd been asking herself: Whether or not she could do as her mother had suggested and try to really see Johnny, instead of being prejudiced by her ideas of who she thought he must be.

She wanted both meanings.

"So." She raised a brow to portray confidence while butterflies landed in her stomach. "Back to my question . . . ?"

Johnny stepped forward, stopping in front of her. His palm cupped her jaw—her imperfect side. "I've never wanted to bring a woman here."

Her mind added the words 'before you.' A thrill ran through her heart.

His thumb caressed her lips until she parted them. As his head lowered toward hers, the smokiness darkening his eyes burnt his mask away. His lips met hers, nibbling lightly, as if tasting her for the first time.

Her breathing quickened and she leaned against him, loving the solid feel of him against her, loving the way his lips moved against hers, leisurely and thoroughly, as if he had nothing better to do than stand there and kiss her forever.

He moved his head an inch away. "I want to keep seeing you."

Happiness flooded her body.

His lips returned to hers. The kiss grew harder, the pressure of his mouth as it moved against hers more demanding—demanding that she open up to him, using his tongue to get what he wanted.

She gave it to him.

Demanding that she give back to him, as his tongue circled her mouth.

She gave back to him.

His hand moved to the nape of her neck, burying itself in her hair before moving upward, pulling her closer. His lips moved faster and more forcefully against hers, his tongue swept her mouth with impatience, as if seeking something more, yet unable to find it. His breathing grew heavier and more ragged, the occasional puff of air caressing her lips, as if desperate to escape his chest.

Tina was equally desperate. She wound her hands around his neck and tangled her fingers in his hair, wanting to pull his head closer, though they were as close as they could get. Her mouth followed the pace of his, moving hungrily against his. Her tongue met his, thrust for thrust.

Suddenly, his pace wasn't enough. She increased the pressure of her mouth against his, commanding him to open wider.

He did.

She pushed his tongue aside with hers and circled his mouth, mating her tongue with his when she desired, beginning her own restless exploration, insisting that he allow it.

He did.

He groaned and dropped his hand from her head, grabbing her waist instead, and pulled her against him, forcing her to feel just what her kiss was doing to him, what more he could give her.

Tina gasped and ground her hips against his,

telling him she wanted it.

He broke the kiss with a grunt. His tongue swirled along her jaw line. "I want you."

You have me.

Johnny dropped onto his knees.

Tina looked down at him, just as she had that night of the fateful dance.

But as his hands slid up her thighs, hooked into the side of her panties and pulled them down, she realized that tonight he had no interest in her stomach, pretend or real. She was about to become the 'dessert' his eyes had been promising her.

Prickles of anticipation skittered across her skin, causing tingles of need.

Johnny pulled up on her ankle, motioning for her to lift her foot.

She did.

He slipped her panties over her shoe, then put his hands on her thighs, pulling, motioning for her to open her legs wider.

She did.

As his mouth touched her throbbing lips, as his tongue darted between her folds, all thought evaporated. A moan escaped her. She jutted her hips forward, pressing her hungry flesh closer to his mouth, as her veins pumped every drop of blood downward, as every nerve in her body came alive and sent sensation spiraling to the juncture of her thighs.

Johnny's tongue fluttered against her clit, up and down and circling and side-to-side, steady and consistent and unrelenting. Her hips bucked. Her breaths exploded from her lungs in loud, jerky pants.

So this is what that feels like.

Like her whole body was awake and throbbing and

aching for what he was giving her.

She looked down at Johnny, at his fingertips pressing the dress against her skin and out of the way, at his thumbs holding her lips open to him, at his head between her thighs.

So this is what that looks like.

Exciting and naughty and sexy as all get out.

At the sight of his eyes, staring up at her, reflecting the heat raging through her body back at her, the sensation that pooled in her stomach and groin raced to her pussy. As his tongue licked and lapped, all the sensation peaked and went still for one second before it exploded. Her body shook and quivered, loosening a loud and long moan from her throat.

As she slumped against the wall with her legs trembling and threatening to give out, marveling over what had just happened, awestruck that Johnny's tongue could wreak such decadent havoc, he stood up. She heard the vague sound of foil crinkling before he was back to her. He shrugged off his robe and slid his hands up her thighs, gathering her skirt at her waist. "Lift your leg. Wrap it around me."

She did.

"Put me inside you."

She leaned back a bit, stuck her hand between them and positioned him, then slid her hips forward.

He gasped.

She moaned.

He grabbed her ass. "Wrap your other leg around me."

After putting her hands around his neck to hold on, she did.

His hands tightened on her ass as he thrust his hips forward and pulled her hard against him.

The shock of it froze Tina's breath in her chest.

Johnny cursed. His body tensed. His fingers dug into her ass.

His stillness was agonizing. Every nerve and cell in her body was alive and pulsing and craving and *waiting* for satisfaction.

Tina pressed her chest against his and pulled him ever closer. She gripped him with her thighs and thrust her pelvis forward, shifting him inside her.

His curse was tortured as his hips bucked. His hands pulled her away from him, then forward, burying his cock within her, then freeing it. His hands and hips set a frantic pace, moving faster and faster. Their bodies slammed together, then parted, then slapped again.

All Tina could do was cling to him, digging her nails into his back, as the heat built within her once more. With each clutch of her hands, each squeeze of her muscles drawing him deeper and closer inside her, each brush of her blemished cheek against his, she kept thinking, *This is what freedom feels like.*

The freedom to be herself, without worrying how she was being perceived.

The freedom to stop hiding.

The freedom to be uninhibited.

The freedom to simply accept that someone—Johnny—accepted her as she was.

The freedom to simply feel . . .

Until her body shook and shivered and climaxed, preventing her from thinking anything more.

As her climax faded away and Johnny no longer pulsed inside her, Tina felt the stiffness in her legs, still wrapped around him. She opened her eyes, taking in the half-filled plates dotting the countertop.

168

"We seem to have a problem eating dinner."

Johnny chuckled. "Is that a hint?"

"Sort of. My legs feel locked around your hips."

"And that's a bad thing?"

Tina laughed.

Johnny kissed the corner of her mouth, then withdrew from her. He picked up his robe and shrugged into it before removing the condom, then tossed it into the wastebasket when he entered the kitchen. He picked up where he'd left off, spooning food onto plates, before lifting the lid on the cake box.

Tina stretched her legs and joined him at counter, standing next to him.

Johnny's laugh sent a buzz of pleasure through her. He was looking at the image on the cake, which featured a muscular guy bent over a pool table. The guy had just 'kissed' the 8-ball with his cue, sending the eight rolling into the 'bed of the table.'

Johnny read the words in the thought bubble out loud. "I kiss great in the bed of the table." His eyes were crinkled with humor, just as they had been in the poolroom. "Awesome."

Tina beamed, pleased that he got the double-entendre. "It's a strawberry and pistachio gelato cake from one of my favorite bakeries. But I asked them to add the pool image."

"Very clever." He flicked his fingertip along the icing and placed it against her lips.

Tina sucked the white icing off his finger. "Yum." She looked up at him, using her eyes to tell him that she found both the frosting and his flesh delicious.

Heat flared in his eyes. He scooped another fingerful and licked it off.

"Umm. Not quite as good as my dessert."

A flare of heat stabbed her pussy. Tina blushed.

Johnny chuckled and, once again, lowered his head. His mouth met hers. His tongue licked hers, giving her a taste of dessert that was a hundred times better than cake.

"You even kiss great *off* of the bed of the table," she said.

"And you wonder why I never let you eat dinner." He kissed her again. Thoroughly. Completely. Possessively.

He groaned. "Dinner. Dinner." He finished dishing food onto the plates, then put one into the microwave, pressed a few buttons, then grabbed a bowl containing salad. "Follow me."

They walked back the way they'd come when she'd arrived—past the table, back to the door and past it. They stopped at the end of the room where panes of frosted glass in dark wood frames extended from floor to ceiling. When they walked through the doorway, Tina saw it was his bedroom.

"Dinner in bed," he said.

Indeed it was. The duvet was folded neatly back at the foot of the bed, while a small square tablecloth, two placemats, and two table settings were placed in the middle. Johnny set the salad bowl between the two settings.

"But you must *un*dress for dinner," said Johnny.

"Undress?"

"Of course. Who gets in bed with clothes on?" The playfulness in his eyes changed to sexiness. "Though I do like this dress." His gaze traveled her body, warming her skin every place that it touched. He placed his hands at the nape of her neck and his fingers worked the knot of her top.

The straps dropped down, leaving her bare to the waist.

Johnny looked down, admiring his work. "Beautiful," he said before leaning forward and taking a nipple into his mouth.

Tina gasped.

Her stomach growled.

Johnny's mouth left her. He grinned. "Another hint?"

Tina's face felt warm. "Ignore my stomach."

Johnny chuckled. "I'll go get dinner. There's another robe in the closet if you *must* wear one."

He left.

Ignoring the lust he'd rekindled, Tina scrambled to the closet. While the thought of eating naked—of watching Johnny's eyes darken, his voice thicken, his cock harden—caused her nipples to tingle and her pulse to skip through her veins, actually doing it would be distracting, not only from eating but, more importantly, from talking. She really wanted to learn more about Johnny. Surely she could manage to focus long enough for a couple of questions.

She traded her dress for the robe and sat cross-legged at a place setting on the bed.

Johnny entered the room with their food.

"Yum," Tina said, tasting the lamb. "This *is* good."

"Umm-hmm."

They ate for a while in silence. This time, the silence was comfortable.

Tina took a bite of rice, delighting in the coconut flavor. Brianna loved coconut. Maybe if Tina made this, she could get Brianna to eat rice. "Thank you again for helping Brianna. She couldn't stop talking about it on the way home."

Johnny took a sip of wine. The way his strong fingers surrounded the delicate glass and the way his lips pursed slightly against the rim as they sucked in a small amount of ruby liquid, then moved the liquid around before swallowing, was erotic, causing arousal to flare in her body.

"She's good."

Who's good? Oh. Brianna. Dancing.

"So you won't tell me what she asked you in private?"

Johnny smiled. "Nope."

Tina smiled. "Well, whatever it was, it has her totally excited. She refused to go to bed without practicing one more time."

Johnny's lips quirked but he remained silent.

"You seem to be good with kids. Do you ever want any?"

His smile disappeared. His eyes remained on his food. His answer was terse. "No."

She hid the flicker of disappointment and changed the subject. "Why did you stop dancing?"

He stilled, then continued eating, though slower. Finally, he said. "As penance."

"Penance?"

"It caused problems, so I gave it up."

"You don't like these questions?" It was the same question he'd asked her when he'd been looking at Brianna's photos.

"No." It was the same answer she'd given. He looked up from his plate. "But I'm trying to."

The flicker of vulnerability that seemed to flash in his eyes before blankness replaced it stunned her. Her heart melted even more. "I understand. There are things I can't talk about . . ." *yet* " . . . either," she said softly. Like what happened with David. Or why she ran away from Johnny's dance. She wanted to tell him, but it just felt too revealing. Too embarrassing.

She lightened her tone. "So what should we talk about?" Again, it was the same question he'd asked her in the same conversation.

He smiled, albeit a small one. After a pause, he continued. "When I told you about the time I went horseback riding, I said I went with a group. I started to say they were boys from the Arapahoe Group Home for Boys. I lived there."

Tina held her breath. He was trying. She didn't want to ruin things by saying the wrong thing, but she sensed he needed encouragement. "How long did you live there?"

"Four years. My mom died during childbirth, my dad took off, and my grandmother raised me. She was great. Died when I was fourteen." He took a bite of salad.

"How awful."

"Yeah. That sucked. So then I went to the Home."

"Oh." *How sad.*

"I met some okay guys, like my best friend, Dwayne. It wasn't that bad." He ate a forkful of lamb before looking up and adding, "And neither was telling you. Bad, I mean."

Her heart melted even more.

He stared at her, his gaze warming until amusement replaced the warmth. "I know that look. Do not thank me."

Tina rolled her eyes. "I wasn't going to thank you."

Smiling, he reached into the pocket of his robe and removed a piece of paper. He handed it to her. "I found this."

One found lint balls at the bottom of their pockets, not a neatly-folded piece of paper. Intrigued, she unfolded it.

It was a printout of a page from a web site. *Dr. Raymond Jennings, M.D., specializing in Port-Wine Stain Treatment and Removal.*

The happiness that had been rushing through her evaporated. The closeness, the connection she'd felt for Johnny vanished. Tina suddenly felt dizzy and as if she were in a tunnel, looking at the paper in her hand from a great distance.

Johnny's voice sounded far away. "Dr. Jennings is a leader in his field. I called him—"

"You called him?"

"Yes. He thinks he can help you."

Tina couldn't breathe.

"He said there are new laser treatments."

Treatments? Johnny was suggesting she needed treatments? Her eyes burned.

"Insurance covers it, too. If not, I can help."

Her eyes filled, blurring the words on the paper. "Why would you do that?"

"Because it's important."

Important to whom?

Finally, she looked up at him. "Why did you do this?" Her voice was barely a whisper.

He looked at her jaw. His hand stroked her blemished skin.

Tina froze.

"Because you should look and feel normal."

The tears spilled onto her cheeks.

Finally, she had been able to let go and just *be*.

Finally, she'd felt appreciated and accepted for

who she was.

Finally, she'd begun to believe that maybe someone other than her family could look beyond her blemish.

Instead, the someone who'd made her feel all this offered to pay for her facial surgery so *she* could be normal.

Just when she'd already started to feel normal. Just when she'd spent hours with him, not even thinking of her face. Not even during sex.

It had all been a lie. He didn't accept her after all. What little acceptance there was existed only because he thought she could be fixed.

Laser, procedures, surgery, whatever. None of it was so that *she* would feel normal. It was because he needed her to look normal.

More tears fell.

"You deserve to be happy."

She wiped the wetness from her face. "I *was* happy."

She got up and grabbed her clothes.

His gaze was shuttered, once again. "What's going on, Tina?"

She left the room without answering.

14

For the thirtieth time, Johnny stared at Brandon's cost and revenue projections for the new show idea—and for the thirtieth time, the figures still didn't make sense. Not because there was anything wrong with the numbers. They were probably fine.

The problem was that Johnny couldn't concentrate on them. In fact, he was having trouble concentrating on anything. He couldn't shake what had gone down with Tina. He'd called her, she hadn't called back, so he'd said 'fuck it' and moved on.

Except he hadn't moved on.

Because he didn't know what the fuck had happened.

He pushed aside Brandon's document, giving up on trying to analyze the feasibility of the show, and turned his attention to the new dance routine he needed to help his men with in thirty minutes. It was an easy routine. Even he should be able to focus on it.

Johnny stood and faced the window. He stared out

over the water while running through the routine in his mind, practicing a few of the steps.

The phone buzzed.

He turned back around, leaned over the desk, and pressed the speaker button. "What is it, Karen?"

"Mr. Guerra, there's a Ms. Edwards here to see you."

Johnny's lips tightened. *Tell her I'm not in.* He would've said it if he'd still been in high school. "Send her back, please."

Seconds later there was a knock at the door.

"Come in."

Tina entered. He glanced at her face, noticing the dark circles under her eyes and the pallor to her skin. His gaze drifted downward, past her breasts, tenting the front of her blouse. He ignored their invitation to him to touch, letting his gaze fall to her hips. She was wearing jeans, similar to the ones—or maybe even the same pair—she'd worn the night he'd met her. Only then, they had hugged her hips and ass the way his hands had itched to. These jeans seemed a bit loose, seeming to hang from her hips, as if she'd lost a few pounds since then.

A flicker of concern melted some of the iciness in his chest.

"Hello, Johnny."

He dipped his head.

"Thank you for seeing me . . . for making time to meet."

So now they were going to be formal, as if this was a business meeting. Was she going to whip out a fuckin' PowerPoint deck next?

"About the other night," she said. "I don't know why you gave me the doctor information but—"

"I thought you wanted it."

She seemed taken aback. "Why would you think that?"

Because you listened to a nine-year-old, dumbass, said the voice in his head that wouldn't shut up.

Don't tell Mommy, Brianna had said.

Johnny ran a hand through his hair. What could he say without giving Brianna away? "Look, I can't talk about this now."

Tina stiffened.

Shit.

"I know you're busy," she said, her voice strained.

"It's not that."

She shrugged. "Never mind. It doesn't matter."

Really? The anger that had been simmering within him sparked to life.

"I am really sorry for my behavior. I shouldn't have left without telling you how I felt and without giving you a chance to respond. But it's not important now."

Anger flared hotter in his chest.

"I didn't come here to talk about that."

Of course not. Because it didn't matter. It wasn't important. *He*—and the whole fucking, fantastic night—wasn't important.

Well, if you didn't come here to talk about that—or to fuck— then why'd you come?

You're being a dick, Guerra.

Johnny forced his anger aside and waited for her to continue, keeping his expression blank.

She fidgeted with her hands before rubbing them, palms down, along the front of her jeans. She bit her bottom lip.

Her movements would have been amusing or even

arousing if he wasn't worried about what was going on.

Worried? What kind of wimpy shit was that? He meant pissed—as in, if he wasn't so *pissed* about what was going on.

Tina took a deep breath, then raised her eyes to his. At the pain and sorrow seemingly reflected there, his chest felt as if a three hundred pound weight was sitting on it. "I'm only telling you this because it's the right thing to do and I already did a wrong thing by not talking to you about that doctor. I don't want to do another one." Her eyes flickered away from his.

He was struggling to inhale, as if his body already knew what she was going to say.

Her gaze returned to his. "I'm pregnant."

He felt his mouth drop open. "What?"

"My period's a week late. It's never, ever late. I took an early pregnancy test, which is 99% accurate. It was positive."

Johnny barely heard her words. His stomach lurched. The blood thundered through his ears.

"I don't want anything from you. I know you don't want children . . ."

His office lengthened and turned wavy, as if he were at the carnival and viewing it through one of those distortion mirrors.

"I should've been on birth control pills. I wasn't thinking. It was an accident and—"

"No!"

He saw Tina's startled expression, also wavy, but still recognizable. The pain that had been on her face when she entered began to change to the hurt caused by him.

She said something but he couldn't hear her. He

wanted to ask her to repeat it but he couldn't speak. All he could do was shake his head before the room totally dissolved and he was in another room on another day.

He opens the door and walks into the house. Past the stove light that is still on and to the refrigerator where he gets a beer. After nine hours at the gym where he works as a personal trainer and four hours at the club where he and the three guys he has hired work as strippers, he is exhausted. But adrenaline is racing through his body for he is also excited. Hot Dreams has just landed its first two shows. He knows this is the start of something big, that he will soon be able to support his family the way he wants to. And maybe, finally, this will make Marta happy.

He finishes the beer and heads to bed. The light is on in the spare bedroom—the room he now uses to practice dance moves but which will belong to his son in a few short months.

He steps into the room and stops, confused. What is Marta doing lying naked on the hardwood floor? Where did she get the red bracelets? What is that she is lying on—did they get a new rug?

And then his eyes make him see what his mind refuses to.

"Marta!" He yells.

She doesn't answer.

Ohfuckohfuckohfuckohfuck!

He runs into the room, slips on the rug that is actually something wet, instead, and sprawls next to Marta. He scrambles closer to her—noticing her eyes are open and vacantly staring at the ceiling, her mouth open as if in mid-snore—and places his fingers against her neck like he has seen them do on TV, but nothing beats against his skin. He removes his fingers, noticing red smudges where there previously were none.

He places his cheek against her mouth.

No air.

He looks at her chest.

No movement.

Someone is chanting, Ohfuckohfuckohfuckohfuck, and he wants to yell at them to shut the fuck up. But he can't. He has to find a phone, has to call an ambulance right away because someone needs to come and save them.

Johnny was jolted back to the present. Tremors wracked his body. He gasped for breath. He kept his eyes closed and waited for his body to return to normal.

When he opened them, he was back in Hot Dreams, in his chair, alone. Tina was gone.

He needed to call her, talk to her.

Later, when he could think.

A door opened, music sounded, the door closed, and then it was quiet.

Still feeling out of it, Johnny looked at the clock.

Shit. He was supposed to be helping the guys with the new routine.

He blinked and shook his head, trying to rid himself of the wooziness and return totally to the present. There was no time for this shit. He got up from his desk, ignoring the shakiness still in his legs, and went to the dance room.

"Okay," Johnny said, after they'd all exchanged greetings. He looked at them, relieved that they were solid, not wavy, which meant the episode had truly passed. "From the beginning."

Nino and Luke moved forward. Brandon and Darrell moved to the side.

"What the hell is this?" said Johnny.

"It's the second set in Caribbean Nights," said

Brandon.

"That's not what we're working on. We're working on the fourth one."

"Oh-kay," said Brandon.

Johnny started the song from the beginning, noticing his hand was still shaking from the flashback that he'd never wanted to replay.

Tina's face, strained and pale, flashed before him.

Pregnant. Tina was pregnant.

A wave of panic rolled through him.

"Nino, what the fuck was that? You dance like the Tin Man. *Roll* your hips."

No one said anything.

Johnny started the song again.

Pregnant.

Husband. Father.

His heart sped up.

The refrain from *Waves* played: ... *and it feels like I'm drowning* ...

Husband. Father.

Without warning, the end of the episode rolled through in his mind:

He yanks his cell phone from his pocket and dials 911. The calm voice tells him someone will be there right away.

Okay, okay.

He throws the phone down, then notices a letter next to her.

Jonathon,
I didn't want this baby but you said giving it away or aborting it was wrong. I didn't want to marry you but you said we should be responsible and do the right thing.

Most importantly, <u>I didn't want you</u>, but you said things would change over time.

Nothing has changed. I tried and, occasionally, I was

even sort of happy. But I'm tired of trying.

I'm getting out of this life I don't want and giving you the life you do want—the one without the wife and baby.

Now you can focus all your time on the only thing that matters—your precious dancing.

Lucky you.

Marta

He notices the bloody prints on the paper in his hand. He notices the pool of blood, smeared from where he slid in it. He notices the blood covering the front of him.

He whirls to the side and vomits.

It finally hits him that his wife and son are dead.

They are dead because of him.

Johnny blinked away the last of the scene, focusing on the present. The shakiness was worse. His head was pounding.

Tina's pregnant. Tina's pregnant. Tina's pregnant.

What the fuck was he going to do?

Nausea churned in his stomach. Sweat dripped onto his brow. He looked at his men, none of whom seemed to have noticed anything. They were still dancing—if one considered that shit they were doing dancing.

"Come on, come on! Luke, Darrell, look like you actually *like* this job. This is not fucking line dancing."

Johnny started the song again.

"Why don't you guys take a quick break?" said Brandon.

"Break? For what? They haven't done shit," said Johnny.

After they'd left, Brandon closed the door and turned to Johnny. "What the fuck is wrong with you?"

"Nothing."

"*Nothing?* You just acted like the world's biggest ass in front of the guys."

"I can't deal with this now."

"That's the problem. You never deal with *your shit.*"

Johnny ran a hand through his hair and turned toward the window, staring sightlessly through the glass as the panic that would not go away continued to send ripples of shakiness through him. "Tina's pregnant."

"Oh."

Father. Husband.

Marta's note flashed before his eyes.

"I can't do this."

"That's all you ever say. What?—What is it you can't do, Jonathon?"

Anger blazed through Johnny. He whirled toward Brandon, jabbing his forefinger at him. "I'll tell you *what.*"

Jab. "I can't deal with trying to make a woman happy."

And failing.

Jab. "I can't deal with an innocent kid dying."

And being unable to save him.

His throat tightened. His eyes filled—he swiped at them in disgust.

Jab. "I can't deal with it being my fault!"

And then, as if a switch had been turned off, the fight left him. He turned away from Brandon, leaning against the window ledge with his head down.

"It wasn't your fault." Brandon's voice was quiet.

Yeah, right. That was so easy for everyone else to

say.

Sometimes, a part of him believed that. He was not responsible for Marta's actions. But he couldn't stop the 'what ifs'. What if he'd been more attentive? What if he'd tried harder? He couldn't stop feeling guilty. Because Marta had been right. He hadn't wanted a wife and child in the beginning. But then he did. And then it was too late.

He was so tired—so tired of feeling it was his fault. So tired of trying not to feel. For the first time since then, with Tina, he'd started to *feel*.

His vision blurred.

"Tina's not Marta. Do you want her and the baby?"

Tina's face flashed before his eyes. Laughing. Smiling. Looking at him with adoration, admiration, desire. Crying, afraid, happy. "Yeah."

"Then you can deal with it."

Johnny closed his eyes and saw Marta on the floor. Something wet hit his cheek. "I don't know how to deal with this shit, Brandon."

He heard Brandon step up behind him seconds before he felt his hand grip his shoulder. "You just did."

15

"I'm pregnant," Tina said, unable to delay telling him any longer. She held her breath, waiting for his response.

Johnny's eyes widened slightly. His mouth dropped open. "What?"

She sped through the explanation, anxious to get it out. "My period's a week late. It's never late. I took an early pregnancy test, which is 99% accurate. It was positive."

The shock seemed to have faded from his gaze. Now, it was unreadable. Not the shuttered gaze she was used to but one that was almost . . . blank.

"I don't want anything from you. I know you don't want children . . ."

She didn't want another child, either. Not now. Not like this. But for one brief moment, as she had stared at the blue lines in the round window of the plastic stick she'd held in her hands, she'd felt a rush of euphoria at the thought of having a baby with Johnny.

Again, she berated herself for being so careless and stupid. With David, she could blame her stupidity on being young—they were virgins and hadn't been prepared, relying on the withdrawal method. But this time, she should have known better than to rely solely on condoms.

"I should've been on birth control pills. I wasn't thinking. It was an accident and—"

"No!"

She jumped, startled by Johnny's outburst. "What?"

He remained silent, staring blankly.

It took her a moment to interpret his silence. "You don't believe it was an accident?"

He closed his eyes and shook his head.

How could he not believe it was accidental? Did he think she'd tampered with the condoms, stuck pins in them or something? Or she'd purposely decided not to take birth control pills in hopes that she'd get pregnant? Or that she *wanted* to be a single mom with two children? Or—

Her breath froze in her chest. Surely he didn't think . . .

"You think I was already pregnant before I met you?"

His eyes remained closed. He remained silent.

How could he believe she would do something like that, try to entrap him? Maybe it had happened to him in the past with other women, but how could he think that about *her* when she'd never given him any reason to think she was like that?

And now, he was refusing to say anything, to acknowledge her, to even look at her.

Just like David.

Her throat thickened.

I will not cry. I will not cry.

Tina straightened her back. She took a deep breath and raised her chin. "I just wanted you to know. I won't bother you again."

She pivoted. As she walked out the door and entered the hallway, she couldn't help herself from hoping that Johnny would call her back.

"Tina!"

Happiness flared within her, then quickly died. "Oh. Hi, Brandon."

His smile faded. "You okay?"

I will not cry.

"Yeah. Yeah. Everything's great." She had to get away. "It was good seeing you." She hurried down the hall.

Luke, Darrell, and Nino rounded the corner in front of her.

No, no, no.

"Hey, Tina," said Luke. The others echoed him.

She returned their greetings.

"We heard Johnny gave your daughter dance lessons," said Nino.

She couldn't bear to think about that now. "Yes."

"Fortunately, he dances better than he plays pool," said Luke.

Nino laughed.

Tina's throat tightened. She couldn't bear to think about Johnny and—or on—that pool table.

"Speaking of pool, you have time for a game later?" said Darrell. "I'd like to see you do a Double Shot."

"No, I—" said Tina.

"How do *you* know what a Double Shot is?" said

Luke.

"YouTube. It's on the Internet. That place you haven't discovered yet." said Darrell.

Luke punched Darrell's shoulder.

Darrell laughed.

Tina would never hear their banter, never play pool with them again, never feel the thrill of being accepted by—and beating—them, nor see Johnny laugh with them or look at her in admiration or—

I will not cry.

"I want you to do that shot, too, Tina. So I can see Darrell lose all his tips by betting against you," said Nino.

"I'm sorry. I have to go."

She rushed down the hall, into the elevator, and down to the parking garage without crying. As she dug through her purse searching for her car keys, her hand nudged the box containing her positive pregnancy test result.

She stared at the box, barely noticing the verbiage boasting that it detected pregnancy sooner than the competition or proclaiming its percent accuracy or stating its expiration date. Instead, she was thinking how she'd brought it in case Johnny wanted proof of her pregnancy, never guessing that he'd want proof that she was pregnant with *his* child.

I will not cry.

She tossed the box in the garbage can by the elevator and ran to her car. She made it inside, managed to start the engine and pull out onto the street before crying.

~~~~

In the three days since Tina had left Johnny, she'd tried to keep her focus on Brianna. She'd helped her

189

with her homework, taken her to ballet classes, baked cupcakes with her and Missy. The only thing she hadn't been allowed to help with was anything related to Brianna's performance. Brianna insisted on everything being a surprise.

In less than two hours, the surprise would be revealed.

Tina glanced around the school auditorium, relieved to see that she didn't know the few parents that had arrived early, just as she and Frances had, probably to pick the best spot to view their child's performance. Tina couldn't stand the thought of small talk, of smiling and asking questions about children she barely knew and frankly, at that moment, didn't care about. It was all she could do to wear her happy face for Brianna. She had no energy to do so with other parents.

A student came up to her and gave her a program. She thanked him.

"Want to sit there?" Frances asked, pointing to the row closest to the front but behind the *Reserved* section.

"That's fine." They made their way to them, then stopped as Brianna came racing down the aisle.

"Mrs. Carson says you're supposed to sit here." Brianna paused to catch her breath. "Since I got the highest score on the spelling test, I begged her to give you guys the front row." She grinned.

Tina smiled at Brianna's excitement

"Grandma, you sit there. Then you, Mom. Is Johnny here yet? He's next to you." Brianna pointed to the seat on the other side of Tina.

Tina's smile disappeared. Pain pierced her heart. "Brianna, I told you he's not coming."

"Yes, he is. He promised." She turned, looking around. "I have to go find Missy."

Tina watched her daughter skip away. "I should never have let her spend time with him." There would be tears when Brianna realized Johnny didn't show. Tina just hoped it wasn't until after they got home.

"It'll be okay. She'll get over him in a few days."

If only it was that easy for Tina.

God, how she missed him.

She pushed the thought out of her mind.

God, how he had hurt her.

She refused to dwell on that.

"It looks like they're selling sodas and snacks," Frances said. "Do you want anything?"

Tina glanced at her mother.

Sympathy shone in Frances's eyes.

"No, thanks, Mom."

Frances patted her on the shoulder and left.

Tina closed her eyes and rested her forehead against her fingers, massaging, as if rubbing would prevent unwanted thoughts. She inhaled a woody-citrusy scent that sent her pulse racing and her breath stuttering in her chest seconds before someone took the seat next to her.

Her eyes snapped open and she whipped her head around.

Johnny?

Johnny!

"What are you doing here?"

"I promised Brianna I'd come." He was sprawled in the seat, legs parted in a wide V. "I need to talk to you."

But apparently, he didn't need to look at her, since he was staring straight ahead.

Just like days ago when she was in his office.

In this case, she was glad. Tina's eyes roved his profile hungrily, taking in his strong, clean-shaven jaw, watching it clench and unclench. Her gaze dropped to his chest, to the black leather jacket gaping open to reveal a glimpse of a purple shirt, unbuttoned at the collar, which made her want to slip her hands under the cotton and caress his neck and shoulder. Her gaze continued downward, stopping at the lean hips enclosed in black slacks and the strong thighs that she had once felt moving between hers.

A shiver of arousal and longing jolted her.

A flicker of anger rippled through her on Brianna's behalf. After practically accusing Tina of entrapping him with a baby, then refusing to discuss it and making it blatantly clear that he wanted nothing else to do with her, he had the nerve to show up here, to breeze into Brianna's life because he'd promised and then saunter out again?

"I don't think it's a good idea for you to be here. I don't want Brianna to see you."

"Let me talk." The words sounded like a plea rubbing against sandpaper. "Then I'll leave before she sees me."

Tina looked at the program now clutched in her hand. She relaxed her fingers. Brianna's performance was last. Johnny should be long gone before Brianna came on stage. To be safe, she could ask him to leave during intermission.

She looked at Johnny.

He turned to her and looked at her for the first time.

Tina inhaled sharply.

He looked awful. His gaze was empty, bleak. Dark

shadows hugged the skin below his eyes.

"Okay." Her voice was a whisper.

He nodded as if to say thanks, then turned around. Resting his elbows sideways on the armrests, he held his fist in his palm and resumed his straight-ahead stare.

"At eighteen, I got a girl—Marta—pregnant." While his voice was dead, a lifeless monotone, his leg bounced up and down. "I married her. I wanted my son to have the parents I'd never had."

Johnny paused. His leg stilled. "She hated me—for getting her pregnant and convincing her to marry me instead of having an abortion."

He closed his eyes. His hands were no longer loosely clasped. Instead, his knuckles were white from the force of his grasp. "She slit her wrists when she was six months pregnant. I found her. *Them.*" His voice cracked on the last word.

"Oh, my God." To see that. To lose his family like that. To have to live with that image the rest of his life. Tina couldn't imagine what that would be like. Her heart went out to him. Her hands itched to reach for him, to smooth her palms over his fingers that were gripping his fist so tightly.

But the tension holding his body taut like a bowstring told her he wouldn't like it. Perhaps even a touch would make him withdraw. So Tina clasped her hands to keep from caressing him. She kept silent, hoping he would continue.

Johnny opened his eyes. His leg resumed its bouncing. "I have flashbacks, episodes. I had one—I saw their bodies again—when you told me you were pregnant. My 'no' was to try to stop it from happening. I wasn't talking to you then. "

"You didn't hear what I said, after you said 'no?'"

"No."

Relief zoomed through her, followed by remorse. "I didn't know that. I didn't know anything was going on."

Johnny shrugged. "It's usually not noticeable, if you don't know what to look for. Not until later, if the episode's a bad one."

That must've been a bad one. "I'm sorry I left."

"I'm glad you did. I'm glad you didn't see it."

So his closed eyes and silence hadn't meant he'd been ignoring her. His 'no' hadn't meant he didn't believe that her pregnancy was an accident. He didn't believe that she'd been lying about it being his child.

Part of her hurt dissolved and floated away.

Slowly, he turned toward her. The emotion in his gaze froze her breath. Pain and need, fear and hope, seemed to war with weariness in his eyes.

The lights dimmed to signal the start of the show.

"I'm scared shitless that—"

A voice boomed over the loudspeakers telling everyone to be seated. Startled, Tina looked around, surprised to see that the auditorium had filled up while she and Johnny had been talking. At the rustle of someone taking the seat next to her, Tina turned to her mom.

"Is everything okay?" Frances said.

"I don't know."

The first group of children came on stage, doing some sort of parody of *Toy Story*. Tina barely paid attention. All she could think about was the man sitting next to her. What had he been about to say earlier? What was he afraid of?

He shifted in his seat.

Awareness tightened her body.

His leg brushed against hers.

Her lungs clenched, stealing her breath and sending sparks of arousal through her, making her want to lean into him, place her head on his shoulder, and place her hand on his thigh and caress his muscles through the fabric.

She moved away. The arousal dimmed but the awareness remained. The desire to touch him thrummed through her.

She tried to focus on the stage. A six-year-old girl gave an off-key rendition of *Tomorrow*.

Once again, questions about Johnny began looping through her mind. Why was he here? Was it simply to explain his actions in the office? Or could he want—

His arm, resting on the armrest, brushed hers.

Desire and need zoomed up to her shoulder, over her heart, and down to her stomach, where they pooled and simmered, growing hotter.

Tina moved her arm.

The little girl stopped singing.

Mrs. Carson announced intermission.

Thank God.

"Oh, there's Lorna Douglas," said Frances after the lights had come on. "I'm going to go say 'hi.' See you later, Johnny." She moved away.

Tina and Johnny sat in silence. Finally, she said, "What did you mean about being 'scared shitless?'"

Once again, Johnny stared straight ahead. This time, his hands were loosely clasped and his legs were still. "I blamed myself after Marta's suicide. I should've tried harder. I should have spent time with her, not dancing."

A light bulb went off in Tina's mind. That's what

he meant, when he'd said he'd stopped dancing as a penance.

"I could've prevented it."

"It wasn't your fault, Johnny."

A faint smile quirked his lips and then was gone.

"When you said you were pregnant, the blame came up, the fear surfaced that I'd mess up again."

He looked at her. The pain from before no longer shone in his eyes, but need still seemed to flicker within, along with the fear. "I'm scared shitless that I'll fuck things up again. With you."

He *was* saying what she had thought. Hope fluttered free, circling her heart. "You're not eighteen, and I'm not Marta."

"I know. Which is why I want you—you, Brianna, and the baby."

Happiness joined hope in its flight through her body. "Oh, Johnny." She wrapped her arms around him and kissed his cheek.

His body remained stiff. Slowly, she felt the tension leave him.

She pulled back. "I need to tell you . . . I'm not pregnant. My period came today. It turns out the test I bought was expired, so it wasn't reliable. But I didn't know that then. I only found out after I left your office and was standing in the garage and—"

She was rambling. She stopped and raised her eyes to Johnny's.

Once again, his eyes widened slightly and his lips parted. The relief she had expected to see was missing. "Oh."

Tina's heart melted into a puddle of mush at his look of disappointment. That morning when her period arrived, she'd felt relief so strong she'd had to sit down. But after hearing Johnny's words and experiencing the depth of his feeling and commitment and remembering her flash of euphoria when she'd first thought she was pregnant, she shared Johnny's disappointment.

"Well. I want you, Brianna, and our future baby."

Tina smiled, then her smile faded at the memory of one unresolved item. "About Dr. Jennings—"

"I don't want to talk about that."

Tina frowned. "What do you mean, you don't want to talk about that?"

The lights flickered, signaling intermission was over. Mrs. Carson asked everyone to take their seats. Johnny faced forward, staring at the stage, fingers clasped, thumbs tapping as if he couldn't wait, as if he hadn't promised to leave.

At that moment, Tina wished she'd remembered to ask him. Instead, she fumed. How could he just turn around like that, without saying a word?

A boy Tina recognized from Brianna's class came on stage, dressed like Elvis. She ignored him, her mind stuck on Johnny. How could he not want to discuss the fact that he'd wanted her to change, to look better, to get her face fixed for crying out loud, because *he* needed her to look normal? How could he dismiss it as if it wasn't important? As if it didn't matter?

Johnny chuckled as Little Elvis started singing *Blue Suede Shoes*.

And now he was *laughing*?

Un-be-lievable.

At Mrs. Carson's announcement of the last act, Brianna, Tina forced her growing anger aside and shifted her attention to her daughter. She took out her phone and started recording.

Brianna came on stage wearing a black leotard, tutu, and tights. Her black hair was pulled severely back and dark powder had been added, making it dull under the lights. Someone had helped with her face, as she had something sparkly added to her skin, a hint of blush, lip gloss, and some mascara.

As *All About that Bass* came on, Tina realized that it was an instrumental version. Brianna started singing and went through her routine pretty much as Johnny had taught her.

Tina smiled with pride. Brianna really was good.

It was only when Brianna got to the third line of the refrain that Tina got what Brianna was doing and saw the changes she had made to the routine. Instead of singing the real lyrics of the song:

I'm all 'bout that bass, 'bout that bass, no treble

Brianna was singing:

I'm all 'bout that face, *'bout that* face, *no* trouble

And each time she got to 'face', she placed her hands near her temples, fingers splayed, as if pointing to her face and moved her neck in that Egyptian side-to-side movement. And each time she said 'trouble', she put one hand on her hip and shook the forefinger of her other hand toward the audience.

That familiar burn, signaling the rush of tears, sparked at the back of Tina's eyes.

Brianna swayed from side-to-side, twirled, all the while making sure the audience knew it really was about her face. And when she got to the line:

I'm bringing booty back, Brianna placed her hands, palms down, fingers straight, under her chin and sang:

I'm bringing beauty *back.*

She looked straight at Tina as she sang it.

Tears formed in Tina's eyes. Brianna had done that for her, to show her in yet another way that she found her mother beautiful. That was the reason for the secrecy, the surprise. That was why she wanted Johnny's help.

Looking through tears, she shot a glance at Johnny, who was watching Brianna with a slight smile on his face.

And Johnny had helped her.

Brianna began the last refrain and when it was over and the applause began, Tina jumped to her feet, clapping and whistling.

Just like Johnny.

Brianna took a bow, then looked at them both with a huge grin and waved.

They waved back.

"Let's give the talented Brianna Edwards another round of applause," Mrs. Carson said.

Tina clapped and whistled again.

After complimenting the other performers by name and commending everyone on their hard work and detailing all the preparation that had gone into the show, Mrs. Carson said, "It looks like the judges have picked a winner." She walked over to the panel of judges and took a slip of paper, then walked back to the center of the stage. "And the winner of tonight's talent show competition is . . . Brianna Edwards."

Tina's clapping and whistling was even louder.

"Congratulations, Brianna. We'd like to present you with a check for $250."

"Thank you." Brianna was beaming. Her smile was bright enough to light the room.

"What are you going to do with all that money?"

Still grinning, Brianna looked at Tina. Her eyes flickered over Tina's face, lingering on her blemish, before turning back to Mrs. Carson. "I'm going to buy my mom the one thing that will make her look and feel happy."

Tina stilled. That was why Brianna had wanted to win this competition so badly. That's why she had wanted the money.

For her.

"I've been saving my lunch money, too."

"How wonderful," said Mrs. Carson. "May you inspire other young people to be so selfless. Let's give this young lady another round of applause."

Everyone did. As Tina's whistling and yelling faded, her throat tightened. The tears she'd been holding back spilled from her eyes, falling against her cheeks. She couldn't believe that all of this had been done with the intent to make her happy—the practicing, the obsession with winning, the insistence on lessons with Johnny. Tina had no idea where Brianna had gotten the idea that she wanted treatments, just as she had no idea where Johnny—

Johnny.

Tina whirled toward him. "You. That's where you got the idea that I wanted to get my port-wine stain removed. From Brianna."

"Yeah. She made me promise not to tell you."

She had gotten so many things wrong, had grievously misjudged him. She looked up at him. He was barely visible through the blur of her tears. "Words don't come close to expressing what I'm feeling but . . . thank you."

His lips curved into a half-smile. Not quite his usual one, but inching closer.

Tina dug a Kleenex out of her purse and dabbed her eyes. "God, all I ever seem to do around you is cry."

"It's part of my charm."

Actually, it was. Johnny's kindness, behind his sometimes-unreadable exterior, continued to surprise and touch her.

"Well, that concludes tonight's show. I want to thank all our wonderful performers and all of you for coming."

The children took a bow. The audience clapped and whooped and hollered. When things had quieted down, Brianna ran over. "Did you see me? I won! Wasn't I great?"

Tina laughed, hugging her daughter. "You were awesome."

"Yes, you were." Frances tweaked Brianna's ponytail. "And modest, too."

Brianna grinned.

"That is so sweet, what you want to give me with your money, Brianna. Let's talk about it later."

"'kay." Brianna turned to Johnny. "Thank you for your help, Johnny. I couldn't have won if you hadn't helped me. And thanks for coming. Mommy said you weren't going to come, but I knew you would."

"You're welcome. I wouldn't have missed it."

"Mom, are you still taking Missy and me for pizza?"

"Yes."

"Whoopee! Let me go find her." She scampered away.

"I'll go with her." Frances winked at Tina and followed after Brianna.

The second everyone left, Tina turned to Johnny.

Her mood became serious. "I'm so sorry about my reaction to Dr. Jennings, for assuming that you really wanted it for you, not me. I've had problems accepting that you accept me, for reasons that have nothing to do with you." Tina paused, then took a deep breath. "I met David when I was seventeen. He was one of the cool kids. Out of nowhere, he started talking to me, liking me. No boy had ever paid attention to me romantically. I was in heaven and in love, or so I thought then. We slept together one time, then I found out he thought I was a freak and had only slept with me on a bet."

Johnny cursed. His look was fierce, as if he'd take David out if he were here.

That made Tina smile, gave her the courage to go on. "I got pregnant. Brianna ended up being the best thing that ever happened to me. But it took me years to get over what David did. To get over my stupidity and my romantic dreams. And I thought I *was* over all of it. Until that dance with you."

She paused to look at him. His look was smoky and warm, as if he were remembering that dance, too. The sexiness of it, the emotion of it.

Tina continued. "I'd picked a husband and father dance routine because I knew you couldn't act that out and make me believe it. But I didn't count on the fact that your pretend feelings would make me feel the loss of those things so deeply. I realized that I still wanted them. And then, when I thought I was pregnant, I realized I wanted them with you. I—"

Before she could finish, Johnny's head lowered to hers. His lips moved across hers, tenderly, as if rediscovering something he had lost and marveling in the feel of it, then more forcefully, as if never wanting it to stop.

Tina's tongue met his, probing and exploring, tasting the delicious spiciness of . . . hope.

Tina drew away. "There's one other thing I have to ask you before you make me forget. Do you want me to get my port-wine stain removed? To try, at least?"

Johnny shrugged. "I don't care, one way or the other. Whatever makes you happy." Her eyes told her he was telling the truth. His actions—his caresses of her blemish, the lack of negative reaction all the time, the desire that she saw in his eyes when he looked at her face—had never lied.

She hugged him tightly. "You've made me start to feel accepted for who I am, despite being different. Which has made me realize that 'acceptance' is more important than 'normal', because I could have society's version of the most beautiful face and still not be accepted. I'm not sure if I want to see Dr. Jennings."

She felt Johnny's shrug. "Okay."

She pulled back. "It may take me awhile to get over my insecurity and to always see the real you, but I promise to try and work on it. But if you can deal with that, I really want to be with you."

Johnny smiled. A real smile that mirrored the happiness in his eyes. "It's gonna be awhile before I'm over my blame thing and can be the man you make me feel that I can be, but if you can deal with that, then I want to be with you."

Tina smiled and tilted her head, placing her lips against his.

"Who's that?" Tina heard Missy whisper.

"My new uncle," said Brianna.

Once again, Tina leaned away from Johnny and laughed. She looked up into his eyes.

He looked down at her with love in his eyes. "No, not uncle. I want to be her father."

And, once again, Tina cried.

ABOUT THE AUTHOR

Rachelle Chase is an award-winning romance author, business consultant, speaker, and model who's appeared on national television—CBS, as well as "The Morning Show with Mike and Juliet"—plus national radio shows, including "Playboy Radio," the "Hip-Hop Connection," and the "Jordan Rich Show."

An excerpt from "Out of Control," a novella in SECRETS VOLUME 13, was used in ON WRITING ROMANCE, published by Writer's Digest Books, to illustrate how to effectively heighten sexual tension in a romance book.

Don't miss the hunky guys competing online to be the hero of HOT DREAMS at www.FindingJohnny.com.

Published works include:

HOT DREAMS
"The Firefighter Wears Prada" in MEN ON FIRE
SEX LOUNGE
A SINFUL STRIPTEASE (The Sin Club Book 1)
A SINFUL PHONE CALL (The Sin Club Book 2)
A SINFUL PROPOSITION (The Sin Club Book 3)
"Out of Control" in SECRETS VOLUME 13

Read more or sign up for her newsletter at
www.RachelleChase.com.

Here's a hot sneak peek at Rachelle Chase's

A Sinful Striptease (The Sin Club Book 1),

available now . . .

PROLOGUE

Transcript of interview with Dr. Tommy "Love" Jones on San Francisco's #1 morning television show, *Wake Up Bay Area:*

Wake Up Bay Area *theme song plays in the background. A red leather couch flanked by two brown suede chairs is situated in front of a floor-to-ceiling backdrop of the Golden Gate Bridge. Dr. Tommy "Love" Jones, wearing a black scoop-neck T-shirt and khaki pants, sits on the couch, arms spread along the back, legs crossed, looking out at the audience with a smile.*

Glass-topped coffee table, empty except for a red ceramic coffee cup, sits immediately in front of Dr. Love.

Wake Up Bay Area *cohost Lisa Mann, dressed in a powder-blue suit, sits in the chair to the right, diagonal to the couch, with her legs crossed, coffee cup in hand, smiling faintly, her profile to the camera.*

Music ends.

ANNOUNCER: Wake up, Bay Area!

LISA: *(to audience)* Good morning, Bay Area. Today, we'll be talking with Dr. Tommy "Love" Jones, host of the popular radio talk show, *The Sin Club.*

(turns to Dr. Love) Welcome, Dr. Love.

DR. LOVE: *(smiles)* Thank you, Lisa.

LISA: *The Sin Club*—such an interesting name. I know our viewers are dying to know the answer to this question: How did *The Sin Club* get its start?

DR. LOVE: *(laughs)* By accident. When I took over the midnight show at KPSX several months ago, I kept the format open. Listeners could call in and talk about whatever was on their mind. Before long, I noticed a pattern. More than half of the folks seemed to be calling in with relationship problems. So I focused the show on relationship empowerment and called the show

The Sin Club.

LISA: *(frowns)* But . . . The Sin Club . . . what does that have to do with relationships or empowerment?

DR. LOVE: *(leans forward, his expression serious)* Most people who called in were unhappy in their relationships, but rather than doing anything about it, they settled—and complained. So I encouraged them to "sin."

What's the accepted definition of "to sin"?—to commit an offense. To these people who were settling and complaining, taking action to solve the relationship problem was offensive to them.

So my definition of "to sin" is to take action. To go after what you want. If you're not happy in your relationship, do something about it. If your partner is not treating you right, don't accept it. If your old methods of getting what you want are not working, try new ones. If you want that man or that woman, go after him or her. *(laughs)* Well, only if you're both single.

LISA: *(nods and sips coffee)* You make it sound so simple.

DR. LOVE: It is. Deep down inside, I believe people know what they want, know what they should do. They know when they should leave a relationship and they know when they should stay. Part of "sinning" is listening to that little voice, breaking out of your comfort zone, and taking action.

LISA: If it's so simple, why is your show so popular? *(leans forward, sets cup on the table, and grabs her notepad, reading notes).* I mean, in less than three months your show has gone nationwide. Your midnight broadcast is replayed twice daily. *(looks up)* Why can't people heed your advice on their own?

DR. LOVE: *(shrugs)* Why do people with a drinking problem join Alcoholics Anonymous? Or people with a weight problem join Weight Watchers? For support. Whenever you're trying to break a habit, it helps to have encouragement. *The Sin Club* is a safe, anonymous environment for people to get the encouragement they need to make hard decisions—and to report back on their success and failures.

With 50 percent of all marriages ending in divorce and about half of those who remain married being in unhappy marriages—not to mention the single folks in bad relationships—unhappy relationships are a big part of American society. That's why *The Sin Club* is so popular.

LISA: Unfortunately, we're out of time. Is there any advice you'd like to leave our viewers with?

DR. LOVE: *(grins).* Yes. Go sin.

LISA: *(chuckles).* All right. Great advice. Thank you for taking the time to chat with us today, Dr. Love.

DR. LOVE: Thank you, Lisa. It was a pleasure to be here.

LISA: *Wake Up Bay Area* will be back after these messages from our sponsors.

Wake Up Bay Area *theme song plays in the background. Dr. Love is leaning forward, forearms resting on his knees, listening to Lisa. Lisa is talking, gesturing with her hand. Dr. Love nods and laughs, then begins talking.*

Music ends.

Cut to commercial.

1

"*Today* is the day to sin . . ." Dr. Tommy "Love" Jones's voice seemed to whisper the words directly into Jessie Anderson's ear.

Jessie turned from the window and frowned at the stereo speaker from which Dr. Love spoke. "I'm *trying* to sin," she muttered.

"Take charge—" continued Dr. Love.

"I am."

"Be bold—"

"I am."

"Do something you've never done before—"

"I am!"

"—something that you've always wanted to do, but never thought you could do. Because you were too scared to go after it. Or scared you might actually get it—"

"I'm not scared I'll get it."

"—Or scared you might *not* get it."

"Yeah, well, I am a bit scared of that one."

"So be bold. Take charge. Do it. Go sin. It's all

about you . . .Tonya M., you're on the air."

Jessie turned her attention back to the window. She parted the gauzy curtain, careful to keep her nakedness hidden. As she peeked outside, she idly listened to the radio show. As Tonya M. described her deep-seated desire to give up psychiatry and become a mortician—and how her career unhappiness was affecting her relationship—Jessie shook her head. Why did the grass always look greener? Here Tonya wanted to flee the living and work with the dead, while all Jessie wanted to do was inject some life, some excitement, some *sex* into a member of the walking dead: Martin.

And today—tonight—was her last chance to save their relationship.

Jessie reached over and switched the radio off. She turned on her iPod. Sade's "Ordinary Love" soothed her frazzled nerves as she gazed out the window, ignoring the beauty of the ocean below. Instead, her gaze sought the backyard of the vacant single-story house next door. She stared intently into the blackness, able to make out the dark shadow that was the gazebo, nothing more.

No flicker of red light.

Jessie dropped the curtain and began to pace, her quick strides causing the flames of twenty candles to flutter erratically as she passed.

Where was Martin? He should have arrived more than thirty minutes ago. She was sure her written instructions had been clear: *Be at the gazebo of the vacant house next door. Flash the light on your key chain at 9:00 P.M. sharp.* Though Martin was a genius with numbers, erotic rendezvous were not his forte. But surely even Martin couldn't screw that up?

Maybe his penlight had gone out.

Heart racing with anticipation, body thrumming with excitement, Jessie rushed back to the window. Was that the signal? She craned her neck. Yes, a definite red flicker. She took a deep breath.

Take charge.

Be bold.

Do it.

Go sin.

Summoning the sexy vixen sleeping within, Jessie smiled in the direction of the signal, and flung open the curtains.

~~~~

Nick Ralston gazed out over the ocean, admiring the moonlight as it bounced off the waves. He loved the sound of the ocean, so peaceful, so different from his life. But that was about to change. Making a fresh start wasn't going to be easy, but he'd taken the first step by buying this house. His house. Well, technically it wasn't his yet, but it would be by next Friday. For added insurance, maybe the "For Sale" sign out front would mysteriously disappear when he left. He smiled at the image of the large sign hanging out of the passenger side of his Porsche Boxster.

Leaning against the gazebo, Nick lit a Marlboro Light. He exhaled the smoke before it could enter his lungs and withdrew the cigarette from his lips, staring at the glowing tip. With a wry smile, he flicked his wrist and sent the cigarette spiraling to the damp grass. He ground the toe of his shoe against it, extinguishing it forever. He sighed. No women, and now, no cigarettes. Which one would prove harder to swear off?

With one last glance at the ocean, he turned to

walk down the path separating his house from his neighbor's, heading to his car. He'd only taken two steps when a movement in the second story window of the neighboring house caught his eye. He glanced up and stopped in mid-stride.

A woman in a red see-through number stood in the window, silhouetted against a backdrop of flickering candles. Nick watched her lean forward and open the window. Muted strains of drums, guitar, and piano drifted over to him, accompanied by a sultry feminine voice. It took him a moment to realize that the throaty lyrics were not recorded with the music, but rather, were coming from the woman herself.

As she straightened, the hot curves of her body were once again visible. The bouncing light shone through the thin material, perfectly outlining the small waist and flaring hips that merged into lush thighs. Thighs that parted and hips that began to gyrate suggestively as he watched.

"What the hell . . .?"

As if in answer to his question, the woman took a step backward into the room. Candlelight illuminated her face enough for Nick to see her lips curl into a seductive smile. He watched her long, slender arms rise above her head, her wrists and shoulders rotating in sync with her hips. Her fingertips slowly traveled down her body, brushing lightly over her breasts, over her stomach, down her thighs, then back up, this time caressing her inner thighs and taking the hem of her gown with them. His breath stuttered in his throat as her hands stopped at her pussy, her fingertips making vertical circles while her hips moved back and forth to meet them.

Nick's hand went to his crotch.

The urge to unzip his jeans and stroke himself in time to the woman's swaying hips surged through him. Instead, he moved his cock to a more comfortable position. He knew he should leave. But, he couldn't. Her hips mesmerized him, keeping him rooted to the spot. Unlike the erotic acts he'd been forced to endure at bachelor parties, this woman's routine seemed... personal. Her movements unpracticed, spontaneous and aimed directly at him, at his satisfaction. He didn't know why or how she even knew he was here.

But, hell, did he really care?

Her fingers stopped their lazy circling, the clingy material dropping back into place around her thighs.

"No . . ." Nick's whisper of dismay escaped him of its own volition.

Ignoring his need, the woman buried her hands in her upswept hair. A quick shake and ebony curls cascaded over her shoulders. She threw her head back, drawing Nick's eyes to her throat, infusing him with the desire to trail his lips along her neck, down to her shoulders, to nibble at her collarbone before licking—

His visual fantasy ended abruptly as her head snapped forward and she crooned to the waning music. Her lips—coated a shiny red that shimmered with each word she sang—plucked a chord tied directly to his cock. A smile spread slowly over her face, as if she knew exactly what was happening to Nick. Then she spun around and sashayed to a chair he hadn't even noticed was in the room. Her back to him, she shimmied in front of the chair, her hands grabbing her ass, squeezing and massaging, her fiery nails glistening with each grasp.

217

Nick licked his lips and reached in his back pocket for the emergency cigarette before remembering it lay mutilated in the grass.

He let his hand fall back to his side.

The music changed to something slower and the piano was replaced by electronic keyboards. As the moody notes of a saxophone cascaded over his eardrums, the woman's hands caressed their way up her back and slid the straps of her gown over her shoulders.

Nick held his breath, waiting, hoping, praying . . .

As if in slow motion, he watched the slinky material slide over her skin, hugging her hips for the briefest moment, before gliding to the floor.

His erection surged against his jeans as he stared at the most perfect ass he'd ever seen. No anorexic model here. This one would give Marilyn Monroe or J.Lo a run for her money. Before he could look his fill at her backside, she turned around and Nick's mouth dropped open.

She was holding a stuffed bear. Only this was no innocent bear from Saturday morning cartoons.

She trailed the bear's face over her body, giving the impression it was bestowing kisses, licking and laving its way across her breasts. She held its head against one breast and rubbed it slightly back and forth.

Nick groaned. An unbidden desire surfaced to feel her hands threaded through his hair, pressing his face against her plump tits, to let his tongue flick across her dusky nipples, to feel them harden in his mouth . . .

He watched her change the bear's position, dragging it across her abdomen, lower, lower . . .

His breath became ragged. "Oh yeah . . . that's it,"

he breathed, as she brought the bear's face to the place that Nick desperately wanted to see, to explore.

Suddenly, she turned around, her back once again to him. The bear's lower body dangled obscenely between the "v" of her thighs as she threw her head back and rotated her hips.

Nick closed his eyes, blocking out the sight of her full derriere swaying back and forth. He inhaled deeply and concentrated on getting his pulse and hormones back under control. He had to get out of there.

Now.

He'd ignore her. He'd walk back to his car, not once looking up at that window. Yeah, that's what he'd do.

He opened his eyes and took his first step with determination. By the second step, he felt his eyes drawn back to the window. Okay, he'd take one last look while he was walking. Before he'd completed his third step, he stopped and gaped at the window.

The bear had disappeared and the woman stood gloriously naked. Her finger curled and uncurled, beckoning. She turned, smiling at him over her shoulder, then moved from sight.

Nick remained where he was, stunned. This woman—this stranger—had just invited him inside.

His first thought was to take her up on her offer, to run, not walk, right up to that second-story bedroom. But the voice of reason intervened, reminding him of his promise:

No women.

Sandy, hooking him with her flirtatious ways, keeping him with her passion and adoration, and sinking him with her lies, had been the perfect catalyst for his vow. While he'd been walking around proud to be her man, she'd been making other men proud—teasing them, leading them on, and sleeping with them.

No. He had no time for women, no time to try and figure out who was telling the truth and who was lying. He was here to focus on work.

No women.

Silently repeating the promise like a mantra, Nick continued along the path and stalked to the front of the house, determined to ignore the images of his naked neighbor and what she might be doing in bed—without him. When he reached the driveway, he opened the car door and paused. He turned around and glanced back at the now-empty window.

His cock still throbbed. His pulse still raced. Curiosity and anger battled in his mind.

Why the fuck had this sexy stranger beckoned *him?*